Claiming his
MAFIA
PRINCESS

A DARK ARRANGED MARRIAGE MAFIA ROMANCE

HANNAH RIO

Claiming His Mafia Princess

FAMILIA VECE
BOOK 1

HANNAH RIO

Chapter One

DALILA

I miss my mother on days like this — on the days when we are all together and I am the only women amongst the men of my family. There's a hollow sensation that creeps in over the holidays, an echo in my heart that no one but her could fill.

I am not alone, not at all. I am surrounded by the men who raised me. My father and my four older brothers.

Love, laughter, and noise resonate through the halls of my father's mansion.

Not one of them is a good man, but they have been good brothers. They're also a bunch of assholes who won't allow me to have any fun.

My friends are all out at holiday parties this week. I am not — I am here at home where they can make sure nothing happens to me. *Dalila has to be the perfect good girl. She isn't allowed friends, or fun, or boys, or kisses* — I am not even allowed a damn dog in case it bites me. As though all dogs just automatically bite.

I roll my eyes whenever I think about how over protective they all are. They don't hear me out when I try to explain to them it feels suffocating. I know they are trying to keep me safe, but what they are actually doing is stopping me from experiencing anything in life.

The decorations I spent all day putting up give everything a festive glow. A golden light makes the house feel warm even though it's fucking freezing outside. Mother Nature is angry this holiday season, and she has been throwing a tantrum for days now. Snow, iced roads and freezing temperatures. It's snowmagedon out there and the weatherman said we are in for at least another week of this madness. The boys have taken over the house, because driving in this shit is dangerous, and I think they're enjoying the free food too much to leave.

"Mas," I can hear my father calling my eldest brother from his office, "I need you in here." God alone knows why he is in there working. It's the holidays. Normal people are shopping, wrapping gifts and spending quality time together. Not my family — the mob doesn't have holidays. Mas' heavy footfalls can be heard as he stomps down the hallway - anything but jolly.

"What?" He roars, and I wonder how he gets away with talking to my father that way. If any of my other siblings tried it, they'd get a backhand. "I am busy."

Busy shoveling food down his throat and tossing back brandy like its soda.

"Tuomo." There's the summons for the next brother — I count silently to myself while I lean against the kitchen counter, waiting for the timer on the oven. It'll be three more seconds until he calls the next one, and in three minutes he'll have all four of them in there. The door will slam, and I'll be left alone in the kitchen.

Three — two — "Rufino."

I knew it.

Celso groans from where he is digging in the fridge behind me. He also knows it is coming. He might be the baby-brother, but they will be dragging him in there with them. My father is in a shitty mood. He has been grumbling all day long. Like a thunder cloud inside the house.

He is almost as miserable as the storm raging outside.

"You know they're going to call you. Why don't you just go?" I ask Celso, who is shoving leftover pasta from lunch in his mouth.

"I'm hoping they'll just get all caught up and forget I am not there. Dad is in one of those moods, so is Mas." He swallows his food then goes on, "Apparently Tuomo was caught behaving badly with some chick half his age."

Sounds no different to any other day. Tuomo has no shame. He will chase anything with boobs. They don't even have to be nice boobs. I shake my head, but I am not surprised.

"At least it isn't one of your friends this time." Celso chuckles. "And they didn't notice you snuck out last night because they were too busy with his lady-drama." Celso winces as his name is screamed out. I smile as he stands, getting ready to leave the kitchen in obedient response to my father's voice.

I did sneak out; I do it often. I just thought I was better at hiding it.

Celso will use this as leverage to get me to do stuff for him — he's a devious little shit.

"Guess they realized you were missing." I say, his comment about my friends has annoyed me. My brothers have this knack of wrecking my friendships by fucking my friends — now we have ground rules. They cannot date my friends. It was my father who actually made the rules after my senior year turned into a bloodbath of bitch fights and bullies.

"Ugh." He groans, putting his food down, he trudges out of the kitchen. I'm alone again, staring at the pile of groceries I ordered for the holiday meals I am going to be cooking.

That's what sisters do — they cook. Since none of my brothers have wives yet, I am the cook. My family is traditional in a lot of ways and one of them is that women belong in the kitchen.

I can't wait for one of them to get married, so there's another woman around to share my load. Housework gets old really fast when they are all here. I prefer it when it is just me and my father. But over Christmas, that is wishful thinking. They 'work' from home this time of year. Given how 'dirty' their fucking business is, that isn't always pleasant.

I pull my long blonde hair up into a messy bun, wanting it out of the way. I grin, knowing my father hates that I dye it blonde. He wants my natural heritage to show through in my dark hair. I want to be fun and carefree and blonde screams both.

Tonight is poker night, and my father is hosting — the place will be crawling with monsters, murderers, criminals and all of the very bottom of the barrel of humanity. They will bet their own mothers in these games. Nothing is sacred to them. Nothing except Cosa Nostra. That comes first. Even though they all hate one another, they are all Cosa, and they are loyal to a cause that'll get them killed eventually.

Men are so fucking dumb.

Do you want to know the reason women don't run the mafia?

Because it's stupid, that's why.

The rules, and the secrets — the part where everyone kills everyone isn't even the stupidest part. I want to kill people all the time.

The stupidest part is the lack of reasoning behind the way they blindly follow rules that are older than my very-dead-grandfathers-father. It's all his fault we're in this shit show. He joined Cosa and now it's our inheritance. Because once you are in Cosa Nostra, you don't get out.

These buffoons often say I am lucky I am a girl, all I have to do is marry the right man and have babies — Yeah. So lucky.

The poker players arrive, one dark blacked out car after another, all the foolish idiots driving in this weather just to come here and clash their egos against the other men.

They dare not miss a poker game.

I have been told to stay out of sight and mind my own business tonight, as always, when they conduct business at home.

Because that's what these 'games' are. Business.

I'm watching from the window upstairs when I see father walking out of the house and getting into a waiting car. He's brave, leaving my brothers in charge with all the heathens here — there is no one to stop them from being stupid now.

I enjoy watching the guests as they come in, all different types of monsters and men. The younger ones are flashy and loud, the older wiser ones are more subtle.

The false smiles, power-play handshakes and occasional genuine man-hugs.

My cousins arrive, already drunk and falling over their feet. They really need to be managed. I heard my father moaning about them over dinner last week.

I'm about to walk away, thinking everyone had arrived, when I see another car stop, and Nevio climbs out. He's in his signature long dark coat. The collar popped up and his hat pulled down low to cover the large red birthmark on his face.

The boys used to mock him relentlessly when they were kids. Now he is one of the scariest men in the mafia. He even looks like a monster — otherworldly, almost as if he's not even real at all. He looks up, and his eyes lock on me for a moment before he smiles and disappears through the front door. I wouldn't want to meet Nevio in a dark alley, or anywhere alone, for that matter. I shudder at the thought of being trapped alone with him in the dark. I'm terrified of the dark, but it would be worse to have him there with me.

The raucous noise downstairs hasn't let up, even though it's well after midnight — my father hasn't returned either. I'm tempted to trip a fuse, so they'll have to leave, but I am afraid of the dark and even more afraid of being in the dark with that many members of the mafia.

Instead, I pull on my headphones and turn Taylor Swift louder than them. I move with the music while reorganizing my bookcase. Then, when there is a lull in background noise, I decide to take a shower and put on some comfy pjs. I'd kill for some hot chocolate, but I was told to stay upstairs.

I'm not very good at doing what I am told — in fact, I am terrible at it. Sick of waiting for their party to end, I sneak down the back staircase and into the kitchen. Quickly warming milk and making myself a cup of hot chocolate, I try to be as fast as I can. Almost escaping unnoticed, I have my mug and a packet of cookies in hand when I turn around and walk full force into Nevio. Of all the people I didn't want to bump into - why did it have to be him?

"Shit." I utter, spilling the boiling hot drink all over my hand. That'll leave a damn mark. "Sorry." I mutter and check that I didn't mess on him. I try sidestep to pass him.

"Hello Dalila," he greets me, his gruff deep voice as scary as his face, "should you be down here? — Alone?" He asks with a sinister undertone in his question.

"It's my house." I sass at him. He smiles and I take the opportunity to get away. Ducking past, escaping him and this awkward situation, taking the stairs two at a time, I can feel his eyes still on me until I round the corner.

My heart is racing, and my appetite is gone by the time I collapse onto my king sized bed. I have never heard Nevio talk before — or even seen him talk. Celso says he's mute. I can now say for sure he is selectively mute.

I heard him talk.

He said my name like it was honey dripping off his tongue.

Chapter Two

NEVIO

The Vece mansion is crawling with every monster known to man. It's like a festival of villains. In this room alone, I can count many men who should be dead or behind bars for what they have done. It's suffocating me being surrounded by so much noise, smoke, and insincere niceties.

Any other place and these men would kill one another without hesitation, except this is poker night — on poker night we *play nice.*

Except, I don't play well with others, not just at poker, but ever.

Earlier I took a walk for air — there is no air in the house that isn't tainted with smoke or cocaine dust.

There is filth for days in here. It's constricting my throat. I'm no better. I have no room to judge them, but I still do. I am not the *same* as them — we may be cut from the same cloth, but I have been starched and ironed hard.

The men are getting more drunk, more hopped up on white powder, more aggressive.

The bets are getting more risky, and I, for one, would like to fold and go home for the night. Yet I stay, because earlier when I went to find air I found Dalila Vece in her silk pajamas. My fucking God, she is a temptation to all of mankind, that girl. They keep her locked away in this gilded cage, but I saw it in her eyes — that girl is wild. A feral little beast just waiting to be set free of her prison.

The Vece brothers will have a husband chosen for her, eventually. It's a matter of time and the right alliance. Her father calls her a menace and says she is a rebellious little devil. I know she has been sneaking out with my younger cousins, doing things and going places where she could get hurt — or worse, hunted.

I know, because I would hunt Dalila Vece.

There are many things I would do to Dalila if I had the chance to get my hands on her — but no one gets their hands on her. *No, she is the ultimate prize.* She was sassy and feisty when I asked why she was down here alone. She shouldn't be down here at all.

"My sister's virginity and fuck it her hand in marriage, too." I almost break my poker face when Masaccio bets her away so frivolously. What the fuck is he doing? He is wasted — he cannot be serious? Many of the men at our table pause, their mouths watering for that pot. It is so incredibly sweet — what is his end game? Or is he just stupid?

"Your father will kill you." The man on his left pipes up, with an indisputable fact, but somehow Mas is unshaken.

"The old man is tired of her shit. This just makes finding her a husband more fun for me. He already tasked me to do it this week, now I can do it my way."

He's wasted. That is the only thought I have right now. They are ready to marry her off before she gets herself into trouble and isn't worth it. A pawn in a much bigger game, I see him and his plan. I raise his stupid bet. If I win, I can make sure the monsters who are worse than me lose.

Many are weary and their pockets are running low, but some go all in — I am one of them. There's a prize I actually want for once. I have money, cars, and all the fine things that this world has to offer. I don't have a wife — and no one would choose me to wed their prized daughter.

I am the faulty son, the one who isn't perfect. I self-consciously pull my collar up on the side to hide the blood red birth mark that shows over it. I'm not the same. I should be my father's pride, his eldest son. Instead, I have been his shame. The one he keeps in the shadows. My physical imperfection made me the second choice. Broken from birth, raised to be the silent killer. I have no voice in my family. I have *one* purpose and it is certainly not to marry a pretty girl.

My only job is to me a monster, the silent shadow of death that these men fear.

Villains like me, we are not made for love, and women, we don't get the family and the feelings you need to be considered a human.

There are advantages to being silent. No one ever sees me coming. They assume silent and deaf are the same thing, shooting their mouths off — I listen just fine. In fact, if you shut up long enough, you hear everything. I know too many secrets, some of them are like lead shackles — others are leverage for days when I need to make myself heard.

I spoke to Dalila in the kitchen earlier. I never speak to anyone. But I wanted to say her name.

Now I am playing a game for her — I will stop at nothing to win her. It is the only way I'd ever be able to attain the object of my affection.

"And then there were three."

Mas says as yet another player folds. Only one of my opponents is not bluffing and I can't be sure my hand will beat his, but I *can* be sure he would break Dalila in a day.

To him, she'd be nothing but spoils of war, a taste of revenge against her father who has wronged many men.

Mas has played right into the hand of his enemy.

That man would be tied to their family forever.

As a man, I have never asked God for anything — he never answered when I was a child, now he certainly wouldn't listen. But I ask, just in case he cares about her, that he allows me to win this hand and save her. Her brother is an idiot who has gambled away his sister's life and body while drunk and high. He should be my next kill, but I can't do that. I won't.

Vece are untouchable.

The room falls silent, the rowdy banter dies down to almost a hush when they realize what is really at stake — and I am sweating at the pressure of so many eyes all on me. I loathe being the center of attention. My skin itches to just throw it in and escape this pressure cooker. They glare. It is my own personal hell.

My collar is too tight, and I can't swallow the fear that creeps up my dry throat. I try to wash it down with cognac. I am so close, but will they really give her to me?

The old man is not here — conspicuously absent — he might put a stop to this. Not because my family is not a good match, but because it is me and not my brother. He's the next in line. I am just the shadow, all I will ever be. Maybe with Dalila on my arm, I could come out of the shadows.

"This is madness." Celso, the youngest Vece boy, whispers under his breath, clearly concerned for his sister, more so than Mas.

Rufino is passed out cold, unable to defend her either. These boys, they have always been on a power-trip; they have an unshakable bind. Tonight I see a crack. Celso is not behind this choice, he is fidgeting and distracting me.

"Why are you doing this, Mas?" He pipes up and his brother gives him a look that makes him shrink away. Masaccio is the boss even though their father is still breathing. He is twin number one, and he leads this family. Tuomo is gone from the party, nowhere to be seen. He is no doubt balls deep in one of the cocktail waitresses that have been serving up drinks, cocaine, and favors all night.

Four brothers — and only *one* is trying to protect his sister. *Disgraceful*. Their mother, sadly, wasn't around for long enough to raise them better.

My opponent scratches his nose, gripping his cards tighter. I know then that I have already won. But I will never allow them to see my victory has moved me. This is business, a tradeoff. A marriage to tie this Vece family to mine for eternity. I cannot imagine my wife is going to come willingly with me.

"Well, Ugly Boy," Ma growls, perhaps only now seeing the stupidity in his gamble. "You have won yourself a wife." He shakes my hand, sealing her fate — and mine. My father will not be happy about this either. Where are all our father's tonight?

Something is not right. Masaccio is too confident, too cocky — what has he done? He is planning something.

I say nothing. These men do not get my words. They are not worth it. None of them would listen. "You can go up and fetch her," he nods to the in-house security to allow me access to the rest of the house, "maybe you can tame the little beast. Careful though, she bites." He laughs.

I bite harder.

Mas is too calm, too confident that there will be no repercussions for this foolish plan.

My suspicions are raised, my guard is up, and I can smell a rat.

I nod, standing up to leave the playing table. I am almost certain I have walked into a trap — but the thing about me is you can't trap a shadow. Even if this is a setup, I am not leaving here without my prize. Security moves out of my path, as Mas escorts me through the bodies, women, and mess to the private side of the house, up the marbled staircase and into the most intimate part of their home.

I can smell her the same way I could in the kitchen. A delicate scent, one that reeks of innocence and fire. Dalila is not one thing. She is, however, mine.

"She's all yours." Mas says a bitter twang in his voice. "Dalila, wake up." He hollers from the door, and I breach the threshold, entering her space.

She sits up in her bed, her silk pajamas have moved, and her breast is exposed. Even in the shadows, I can see her sweet, pert nipple.

"What the fuck, you asshole? I am sleeping. Take your bullshit party downstairs." She sasses at her oldest brother. He growls.

"Party is over, and you are going home with your husband to-be here. He won you fair and square. I will have your things sent over tomorrow." Mas is emotionless when he speaks to her, unaffected by her cheeky tone. He is cold and completely calm. Dalila laughs, her sweet giggles bubble up from her belly as she rolls on her bed as if this is a joke. "Whatever. Get out of my room."

"You can stop laughing." Mas says.

"You going to marry me off to the silent, ugly guy?" She asks, realizing Mas is not joking at all, "are you fucking for real?" Dalila looks scared now, her bronze skin turns ashen.

"Mas, what have you done? Dad will never let you."

"Dad is on board with this. It is time you got married. It will get you back under control." He looks at me, silently handing that responsibility to me. "Nevio is from a good family, and he will make sure you are cared for."

"I know what he is!" she says, her pitch higher now, "you have lost your fucking mind if you think I am going to marry him. Go down there and pick another. Someone else. Anyone else."

"He won you. It is not about picking." Masaccio isn't budging - not emotionally or physically, he stands dead still.

"Get up, put on some shoes, and do as you are told, Dalila." Her tears shimmer in the moonlight where it pours in through the window. Her sweet tender innocence shines through over her feisty fight, and I watch her break into a million pieces as she stands up and obeys her brother. Destroyed by his brutal betrayal. Could she ever have seen this coming? Someone she loves throwing her to the wolves like he did downstairs.

She's lucky it was me that won. She's lucky it wasn't one of those demons who would have torn her apart. Literally and figuratively.

I will put her pieces back together and show her how precious she is. If I do nothing else, I will love Dalila Vece, because she is mine. I won her fair and square.

"I hate you." She seethes at her brother, standing beside me in her pajamas and a pair of sneakers. Her hair in a messy ponytail and her face clear of all her usual makeup. The most beautiful prize in the world. "Celso!" she shrieks at the top of her lungs, but no one is coming to save her from me.

"You better take her before she creates a scene." Mas speaks to me and I nod, turning to her. She is crying and when I step closer, she balls her fists and pummels them against my chest. It tickles — she hits like the pretty little girl she is. I lift her over my shoulder in one quick move. She screams and kicks, but nothing could stop me from taking her now.

Now I have touched her — she is mine.

Chapter Three

DALILA

The tall man with long dark hair covering face hauls me from my bed, out of my house and into the freezing night air. He doesn't even feel my punches and kicks and the savages in the house all act as if no one sees this happening.

I'm just a sideshow in their game night — where the fucking hell are my other brothers? Why is no one stopping this? Where is my dad?

My tears roll the wrong way down my upside-down face and land between his strides on the driveway. The blip of his car as it unlocks is loud in the deathly silent night air. He smells like soap and cigar smoke, mixed with the sweetness of whiskey. His shoulder digs into the soft part of my stomach, and his grip around me is unwavering.

Nevio is quiet. I can hear his thudding heartbeat and the sound of his feet, but not a word comes from his mouth.

Not once in all of this did he even talk.

"Put me down." I screech, trying again to plead with anyone with reason — but I am not sure the silent shadow of a man can be reasoned with. I'm still reeling with shock when he offloads me into the front seat of his blacked out SUV. He leans over me to put my safety belt on, his face so close to mine.

He pauses, a breath away from me, and looks me in the eye. I see a villain, a monster, and he sees my fear. My heart stops and starts, and my breath catches. Nevio is looking at me — no, *into* me - but - his eyes are *softer* than a villain's eyes should be. They whisper a silent apology to me.

But it doesn't stop him. He is still taking his prize.

When the belt is clicked over me, he cups my face in one of his enormous hands. His long hair hangs in his face, and I see the blood colored stain on his neck that I have heard whispers about all the years. The mark of the devil, the superstitious ones call it, my mother was part gypsy, and she believed that is what it was. My oldest brothers bullied him when they were kids, but Nevio became a killer that even the strongest men fear now.

In that second looking at me, time freezes, my panic turns to calm — somehow I know he will not hurt me. At least not here in front of Mas, maybe later, but for now I see his remorse. His silence speaks for him. His hand is warm against my wet cheeks, and his thumb wipes away a stray tear before he moves away and licks it off his finger.

That should scare me, but in some confused state of mind, it turns me on. *I think my mind has snapped.* Nevio leans in and kisses my tightly sealed lips. His breath is warm, and his lips chapped against mine. I don't let him in, but when he pulls back, I can taste him. I'm not ready to give myself to him, or anyone. Not like this.

My brother *bet me in a poker game* — something I never ever dreamed would have been possible. Not even in my wildest nightmares could I have come up with this.

The betrayal cuts deeper than any knife ever could. Masaccio might as well have stabbed me himself.

When Nevio slams the door I jump, but I do not run. I know better than to think you can escape the Mafia. I have been a prisoner all my life. I will never get away.

It is snowing again, and wind howls and whips it up as we pull away from my home — I can see the flashing of the Christmas tree lights in the mirror as I look back. The decorations I put up. The warmth I added to that house.

Celso is on the front steps. I can see his face as we're torn away from one another.

I feel angry at him. Where was he when I needed him? Why did he not stop this? How could they?

"It could have been worse." I jump at the deep sound of Nevio's voice. I don't look at him. I don't want him to see my tears as they stream down my cheeks.

I'm terrified. My entire life has just been ripped out from beneath me. I was literally taken from my bed in the dead of a winter's night - and he thinks it could be worse?

"It was me or Lorenzo, and I know you know what he does to his women."

I swallow the vomit that claws up my throat. Would my brother have given me to Lorenzo? Is he really that cold?

"I made sure that I won," He says, driving slowly through the thick weather, "I will not hurt you, Dalila."

It's too late. I am hurt beyond repair by the betrayal of my brothers.

It's like the world has been flipped upside down.

Nevio is speaking to me, and I am the silent one.

The roles flipped on their head. I have lost my voice. I was given no chance or option or choice in this matter — if I was, it wouldn't have been this man. "But I will also not let you go."

The words crush the last sliver of soul I had, and I close myself up inside mind. I put up every defense I have and wipe away my tears — they will not break me. No one will break me. No one can hurt me if I am numb.

"Where would I go?" I turn and glare at him, my fear and pain turn to anger and murth. "If I got away. Where would I go? Back home? What home?"

He just looks at me, then back at the treacherous road ahead of us. I don't even know where he lives — the man is a ghost. The quiet inside the car swallows my emotions whole, and the air takes on my anger, making it thick and harder to breathe. When the weather thins out slightly, Nevio takes one hand off the steering wheel and puts it on my exposed thigh. I was so angry I didn't even feel the biting cold as I was dragged outside half naked.

His hand feels hot like a branding iron against my clammy cold skin, yet goosebumps of pleasure, not cold shiver across my body. Why does his touch feel good? I should want to shove his hand away, but it feels good — like a comfort that is both frightening and familiar.

Squeezing my legs together, I fight against my own conflicted mind and tell myself this is just shock. *I am in shock*. The car slows down and rolls to stop outside a massive gate; it is covered in icicles, and I can see the snowflakes falling in the glow of the headlights as it opens. The path ahead is unlit, black and as if I am being driven straight through the gates of hell into an unknown abyss.

Nevio pulls his car into a garage, and the doors close behind us, plunging the place into darkness, his hand still on me. "Welcome home." Nevio's voice vibrates around me. I gasp. His hand slides higher up my thigh, and I can feel his body heat as he leans closer to me.

Frozen, I don't pull away, I just sit there trembling inside and out.

This time, when his lips touch mine, I have no fight left. I give in to his warmth and the taste of expensive liquor that coats his tongue. There is no light. I can't see his face, or the kiss of the devil — but I can feel his intentions.

I allow myself to kiss him, to get lost in this darkness where I cannot see the face of the villain who owns me now. Here in the pitch blackness he is just a man, that is kissing me, his hand dangerously close to my silk shorts, ghosting over the part of me that has betrayed me more than my family. *I feel the clench of desire.* The *want* for him to touch me — but no one has ever touched me besides *me*. One fingertip softly brushes the silk and I moan into his open mouth.

Oh. My. God.

Nevio possesses me in the darkness. He doesn't need to restrain me — I willingly cave into the feelings his kiss stirs inside me. No one has ever been this close, been able to kiss my breath away and then resuscitate me with theirs.

I have had dreams about the man I'd end up with — that he would know how to make me feel good. I never imagined it would be a villain who won me in a poker game.

Nevio makes a sound that ripple through me like a growl.

The vibration only turns me on more. My pussy has only ever been this wet when I play with my secret toy. The one I keep in the drawer beside my bed. I use it when I have made myself all worked up reading sexy books. *I may be a virgin, but I am not innocent.*

My skin ripples with goosebumps, and I want to stay in the dark, in this kiss forever. If the lights turn on, I will have to face the reality of Nevio and how I ended up here. I don't think I want to know why my brothers did this — that thought is more frightening than Nevio's hands on me.

Something has to be terribly wrong.

But it feels good, the way his lips taste, and his hands command my body. I like it, there is a warmth building inside me.

Nevio stops, pulling back just enough to catch his breath. My God, that kiss was like nothing I have ever felt before. I shudder just thinking about it, and immediately I want more — I don't want him to stop kissing me. It's like I need him to touch me so I can forget that this is all real.

"It's past your bedtime." He growls, and I shiver at the vibration of his voice so close to my ear.

When the car door opens and the interior light casts a golden glow onto his face, I see him, really see him. I have never looked at Nevio. It is rude to stare and it would have been staring. Only because before now I would have looked at the red mark spilling out over his collar, not into his eyes, or at the way his hair falls into her face, which is younger than I thought it would be up close.

In the haze of post-kissing bliss and the dim light, he isn't half a monster; he is actually quite beautiful. The man looking at me doesn't look like the killer I know he is.

Chapter Four

NEVIO

If I don't stop myself right now, I will deflower Dalila right here in the front seat of my car, and that isn't what I want.

She's worth waiting for, taking my time with, she isn't going anywhere — she is mine and I plan to enjoy her.

She tastes like sin, and I am hungry for more.

I open my car door, stepping out into the garage. The lights are off, but I know my way around. Walking to the passenger side, I open the door for her and hold out my hand to help her climb out. She stumbles, slipping on the wet runner-boards, falling straight into my arms. Her half naked body pressed into mine. I suck in a breath, praying for self-control. Lord help me, I do not have many virtues, but I want to wait.

Dalila is here, and I do not want her to hate me. I want her to know that I saved her from far worse.

No one has ever been inside this house and left again — not alive, that is. She rights herself, still crushed against me. She must be freezing in those thin pajamas. We need to get inside where the heating is on, and I can decide exactly what it is I plan to do with Dalila Vece. Ushering her through the security door that leads from the underground garage up into the main house, I notice just how petite she is beside me.

The house is warm, my tense, stiff body relaxes inside the comfort of my sanctuary. Her eyes dance around, looking at everything. She folds her arms over her chest to warm herself up. Her hair is a tangled mess from sleeping and my hands in it. She looks sexy and scared all at once.

"It's late." I say, because it is, but also because I have no idea what else to say. "We can go straight to bed, and I will make sure you get your things tomorrow." Her big green eyes glitter up into mine, and I can see the tears shining in them. I don't want her to cry — or be afraid. For just once in my life, I want someone to want me — to stay the night and not turn their eyes away from me when they see me.

"Where is my room?" She asks me, her voice shaking as if she shivering.

"With me," I say without hesitation. If I am doing this, then there will be no half measures.

"You're going to be my wife. There is no point in having separate rooms." There's a flash of fear in her eyes before she nods. Mafia daughters are raised not to ask questions or argue — she's a feisty brat who doesn't always follow the rules, but I think she is too afraid to push me. "Come, Dalila, you don't need to be scared."

She is terrified. I can smell fear at fifty paces — I can't blame her. She wasn't prepared for tonight's events. Neither was I. I still can't quite fathom why her brothers did this, or where our fathers were and how come hers didn't stop me taking his prized daughter. Something still doesn't feel right. I'm uneasy about my victory.

"Are you going to hurt me?" She asks softly.

I am not stupid. I know my reputation. I may be quiet and unassuming, but everyone knows how many corpses have my personal stamp on them.

"No," I have no intention of hurting her, "I will not hurt you. A husband's job is to love and cherish his wife, never to hurt her."

My day-job and my responsibility to her will be two different things.

"Are you going to kiss me again?" She whispers, stepping closer to me.

"Yes," I breathe, "I hope to kiss you many more times, Dalila." Her cheeks blush a soft pink, and her lashes flutter as she looks down instead of into my eyes. I won't hurt her, but I do plan to enjoy my wife — and I hope she will be willing.

"Will you kiss me again now, please?" She says with her eyes closed. She's a gorgeous woman, and I want nothing more than to kiss her again right here. I'm afraid if I do though, I may not stop at kissing her — the temptation is too much.

"Not now," I whisper dangerously close to her lips, "Dalila." Her name is like syrup, sweet on my tongue.

We're both tired, and it's late, and we are overwhelmed by our new arrangement. I don't want to take this too far and regret it or scare her. I don't kiss her, but I wrap my arms around her and lift her up in my arms, carrying her like the precious gift she is, across the house to my bedroom.

Her small body fits snug against mine, she's soft and I'm hard — she is beautiful and I'm the beast men go to bed and have nightmares about. She smells like hot chocolate, sweet and warm, and my body reacts to just how right she feels in my arms.

The small lamp beside my bed is the only light in the room — I loathe bright lighting or mirrors. My home is devoid of both, I do not need to see myself clearly, I already know how ugly I am. Dalila lets out a soft sigh when I put her down gently on the end of my bed, her legs dangle over but are too short to touch the floor. She kicks off her sneakers and looks up at me as I strip off the suit I had to put on to attend poker night.

At home I prefer sweat-pants, a turtle-neck sweater and clothing that is comfortable over the starch of a shirt collar. I unbutton the last button and peel off the only thing protecting me from her eyes; the shirt covering the dark red mark that stretches from my neck down my chest. The very thing that caused my father to reject me from the moment I was born — I'm inferior because I am not perfect. And my father and brothers never missed a chance to remind me of that.

It's hard to love imperfect things.

I hear her gasp when she sees it. I know the look in those eyes all too well. I don't know why I undressed in front of her — I have never allowed anyone to see me as naked as this. Yet with her, I have no desire to cover up. She gets all of me. Since I expect to have all of her. Instantly I feel exposed, vulnerable and hoping that she will see *me*. Not *just* the blood colored stain that makes me into a monster. "It's bigger than they said -" she whispers, sliding off my bed and taking a step towards me.

I stop breathing when her delicate fingers trace the edges of my birthmark, as if she is committing the shape to memory. "I only ever saw the part your shirt doesn't cover." Her eyes meet mine, and I want to close them and shut her gaze out so she can't see how much this is hurting me.

"Stop." I whisper breathlessly, "Please, Dalila." Her fingers stop moving, but they are still touching me — frozen there over the part of me I have wanted to cut out with a knife more times than I can count. Scars would be better than this splattered stain.

My eyes close as my heart thunders in my chest. She's too good for me.

This is a dream, and what happens when I wake up tomorrow and it's all shattered into pieces around me?

When her soft lips touch the spot right over my heart, I have to bite back the sounds that slowly start erupting from deep within me. Her tenderness covers her fear. "There, now I have kissed the devil right back." She says, and I shiver at the way her breath dances over my bare skin.

My phone vibrates in my pants pocket, breaking the spell between us. I step back and turn away from her to see who it is.

> **Masaccio Vece:**
> Take care of her. I hope she doesn't hate me. I had no choice. This was the best way to protect her from what was coming.

I knew something wasn't right, that he was acting like a lunatic. This had to have been planned. I reply to his text, assuring him I will keep her safe. His reply makes me wonder what or who exactly he was protecting her from.

> **Masaccio Vece:**
> You need to marry her, not in a month. Tomorrow, I have arranged for the priest. He will be waiting for you two in the private chapel at midday. Don't wait Nevio, I am trusting you with her.

"Who is that?" She asks me, "You tensed up the minute you got that message. Who is it?"

"Your brother," I answer, "something is wrong, Dalila. He says that we can't wait. We have to get married tomorrow. That he hopes you don't hate him. He was protecting you from something. He won't say what."

I watch her expression change as she thinks about what I've told her. She swallows, and I trace the path of a single tear as it falls down her cheek. She nods her head.

"I'm sorry I called you ugly," she says. "I was scared and upset. You said you won't hurt me, and I trust you. Mas wouldn't have chosen you if he didn't trust you too."

Dalila looks down, and then straightens her shoulders, looks me in the eye, and I watch her push her fear and anger away.

"I will take you to get a dress in the morning. We are going to the chapel at noon." I say, tipping her chin up with my finger, "Dalila, this may not be the conventional way to do it, but you're mine now. I will keep you safe, and I will give you my entire world. But you need to give me the same. All of you—" I don't finish my sentence because she pushes up on her toes and kisses me.

Chapter Five

DALILA

My fear melts away when I taste him again — my anger dissipates, and all I can feel is his heart hammering against his chest in time with mine.

Nevio is a killer, an enforcer, while he looks quiet and unassuming. I know who this man is, and I know I shouldn't want to kiss him.

Everything inside me says I should kick, scream and fight my way away from this, but I can't make myself let go of him. In his arms I feel safe, as if this monster would murder anyone who touched me, but he'd never lay a finger on me.

My skin burns like fire with need when he touches me. His cock is hard, strained against his pants. There's no hiding it when he pulls me against him and deepens the kiss that I started.

Tomorrow I'll be married to the man the devil kissed.

Nevio pulls me up into his arms, against his hardness, and takes me to his bed, *our* bed now. He puts me down tenderly, kissing me, his hands roaming over my silk pajamas. Teasing me, making me buzz with need. "Please." I hiss into his kiss. I want more. "Nevio, please don't stop." I beg, breathless — desperate.

"Not tonight, Dalila." He growls, burying his head in my neck, "Tomorrow night, I will make you mine. After we're married." Now he's a gentleman, what the fuck, he kills people and in bed he wants to be chivalrous.

"I don't want to wait anymore." I say, hoping he will give me what my body is so desperately craving. Nevio pauses. He looks down into my eyes and smiles at me. It's a devilish smile, one that reveals parts of him no one sees. Playful and mischievous.

"Patience," he says, "I will make you feel good, but I am not taking your virginity tonight." My body shivers at the low timber of his voice. Then his fingers slip under my shirt, his warm hands against my skin. I moan at the sensation.

My nipples pebble hard when the palm of his hand grazes over them. It's like a tingle that turns from painful to pleasurable. I want him to stop, at the same time I want more — God, please don't let him stop.

He pulls my top off, over my head and throws it off the bed behind him. On his knees towering over me, Nevio looks at my exposed body. A hunger in his eyes that I've only read about in the books in my old bedroom. Then he leans down and kisses me. Harsh, rough — his need matching the desire firing inside me. He kisses down my neck, a trail of heat making me writhe beneath him, wanting so much more.

When he suckles my nipple into his mouth, my back arches off the bed and I let out a cry of pleasure. His tongue swirls around the sensitive bud, making my pussy wet. He keeps kissing me, lower and lower, down my belly. When he reaches the top of my shorts, I hold my breath — wanting more but afraid of what more is.

No man has ever touched me this way, and while I am hot with want, the shiver of fear still lurks beneath the surface. He hooks his finger into the elastic and pulls them off, shoving them down my spread thighs. They're not off, but I'm naked and exposed to him, those dark blue eyes taking mental pictures before he kisses my inner thighs.

My pussy clenches with each kiss, and when he nips gently, biting me, I moan his name. My whole body shivers and shakes. I have read about this — in those same books — but never imagined how intimate it would be to have a man down there.

His face is so close to my most private parts, I'm shy, but so turned on I can't stop him — so I lean back, turning my face into the pillow so I can't see the way his eyes glaze over my body.

My fingers grip the soft cotton bed covers. When his tongue touches my clit, my whole body jerks. When my legs try to close on their own, he forces them apart with his hands holding me open and exposed to him. "Nevio," I cry softly, "I haven't—" he pauses when I stop talking. "No one has ever touched me — there."

The pause only lasts a moment before his mouth is on my pussy again, licking — teasing — making me want to close my legs. My orgasm teeters on the edge and every time I think I am going to come, he slows down again. The sweet torment is driving me crazy, the inaudible words coming from my mouth sound like someone else.

Nevio doesn't stop. His tongue rubs against my throbbing clit and when he slides a finger into my tight pussy, I am no longer in control. My entire body shakes and gives in to his caresses, and my pussy clamps over his finger as wave after wave of pleasure engulfs my body entirely.

I gasp and then I can't breathe.

It's more intense than it ever felt when I played alone.

It's more intense than any of those books described.

Nevio chuckles, low and dark, and crawls his way back up over my body.

His cock is throbbing. It's so hard against his pants.

I want to feel it.

I reach out and run my hands over the bulge as he lies down next to me.

He grabs my hand, shuddering under my touch.

"Don't," He says, his voice thick with warning.

"Why not?" I pout, not think it's very fair of him to deny me.

"Because if you touch me, I won't be able to control myself. I want to wait. Until tomorrow night."

"But—"

"Dalila. I said no." His voice is sharp and scary.

I bite my lip, staring into his eyes. The blue seems to change from dark to ice, depending on his mood.

"Ok." I say after a long pause.

My body feels like it's glittering, like my skin is alive, after what he just did to me.

I am satisfied *and* left wanting more at the same time. I just can't even imagine what more feels like. If that is how incredible playing feels, what does sex feel like?

I lie my head on the pillow. It smells like him. Soap, cologne. His skin.

I'm nervous to reach out and touch him again after he told me off the last time, but I don't want to feel so alone right now.

I keep my hands to myself, but I shift closer to him. My body curves against his side.

He sighs, then wraps his arm around me, holding me against his chest where I rest my head and close my eyes.

It is late. It's been a long - and crazy night.

I can't believe everything that happened.

Chapter Six

NEVIO

Sleep eludes me, and I am up all night — I've never spent a night with someone in my bed.

Never mind someone so beautiful.

I can smell her and feel her warmth. It's like lying down with the devil and having to resist the temptation of everything you ever wanted right there.

Her brother's messages are on mind. He's not been online again since then. In the pit of my stomach is a growing feeling that something far bigger than a secret wedding is happening. It's as if this was all carefully planned without me even knowing I was involved. It's like he knew I would win the card game. He was confident and cocky about it - because he knew.

I roll over and stare up at the ceiling, wondering if I should call my brother and ask him if he knows anything. Then he'd make me feel like I don't deserve her, or worse, try to take her from me.

No. I have to marry her first. I have to seal the contract with our signatures in a church under the eyes of God.

I can manage a wedding, and a wife — I manage other more dangerous shit every fucking day of my life. They'll call me in the morning. I am sure that news of my win has spread like wildfire through the 'prayer chain' that is mafia gossip.

I glance to where she is asleep beside me and wonder what I did to deserve this luck? Someone has given me a gift, and I will take care of her. I won't take this for granted.

Kissing Dalila was like drinking from the fountain of youth. I am alive — awake for the first time since I can remember I have an excitement brewing in me like a wildfire, spreading through dead bush, igniting it so that the old branches can be burned away, and new ones can rise in the ash.

I used to feel this way before a kill — lining up the sight of my rifle to perfectly eliminate my target. A thrill that makes my blood run hot and cold, one that caused a hunger in me that was never satisfied. I'm afraid the hunger for her will be even worse, that the more I have, the more I will want.

The sun comes up slowly, and the shimmer of dawn lights the room. I want it to slow down. Today has arrived too fast and with it the interference of other people. But, also, I am in a hurry to make her my wife. If I marry her, no one can take her from me. And if they try, they will learn why I am the killer and not the leader.

Trying not to wake her, I swing my legs over the edge of the bed, stretch out my tired muscles and drawing in a long breath. I'm going to be a husband, and I plan to make this rushed wedding as perfect as I can in only a matter of hours. Taking just my phone, I sneak out of the room. I know how to get in and out of places without being heard.

In the kitchen I turn on the coffee machine and wait for it to gurgle to life. An espresso for breakfast keeps the blood pumping. It's early, but I haven't got time to hang about and wait all day. I pull up my sister's number and hit call. We're close — well, close enough that I know she will help me without causing utter chaos. If I call my mother, she will want to wait and invite the queen. I think she thinks I was interested in men — not woman — on the not-so-straight side of life.

Mas was clear about this being urgent — no waiting for the queen, and certainly no time for my mother's high drama reactions. "You better be bleeding if you are calling at this hour." She croaks into the phone. I forgot the ladies have a 'girls' night' when we play poker. She's probably hung-over, and half dead.

"Better than bleeding." I say with a smile she can't see.

"Dead then?" She jokes, "your ghost is calling to wake me." I laugh. My sister isn't like my brother. She understands me. She knows how to make me laugh. She sees through the flawed skin I am trapped in.

"Better than dead," I can't stop smiling, it's weird, "engaged. And getting married in about five hours, so wake the fuck up and get over here. I need help."

"I need more than a lame ass joke to get me out of this cozy bed. Are you high? Drunk? Did you get hit on the head?" She sounds genuinely worried now.

"Lucia, get over here and I will explain everything." I say, "do *not* tell anyone, for now, this is a secret."

"If I get there and you are about to kiss-the-bride with a blow-up doll, I am having you committed into a psych ward. Do you hear me? Ugh. Fine, I'm coming. Dad isn't home, and mom drank her body weight in chocolate tequila last night. She'll be comatose until at least three."

Thank God for small mercies.

"Wear something pretty, please." I add, she sounds like hell, she'll look like hell. "There will be pictures taken."

"You are so fucking lucky I love you." I can hear her groaning, "Thirty minutes. And for the record, you will owe me huge." Oh, I have no doubt I will pay dearly for this favor. I pour a second coffee and wait for Lucia to arrive.

"Nevio," her voice could wake the dead. I rush to intervene before she yells again.

My finger to my lips I shush her, "what the fucking fuck is going on?" she whisper yells at me. "Where is dad? Did he sleep here?"

I shake my head and usher her into the kitchen to explain what is going on.

Lucia might be a brat, but she is a smart brat — nothing gets by her unnoticed. As I tell her the story of last night, her frown lines get deeper. "Dalila Vece is in your bed, and you are going to marry her at noon?" When she says it slowly like that, it does sound rather insane.

"Yes, and yes." She nods, then shakes her head. "Oh God, Lucia, please just get me a white dress that will fit her, some flowers and two rings. That is your assignment. That and shut your trap and do not tell *anyone*."

"Those are very conspicuous purchases. I won't actually need to *say* anything, and people will be talking." She points out.

"Send someone then." I sigh. She is going to waste time. "I need to get a suit and make sure of a few details." Like calling my father, who is probably in the city apartment with his whore.

"You're not joking, are you?" She asks again to make sure, and to answer her, all the proof she needs - Dalila walks in with bedroom hair and tired eyes. "Oh, ok. You are serious. Fuck."

My sister's jaw drops, then she snaps back to reality and greets Dalila.

"Hi," Dalila says shyly, walking towards the smell of coffee, and towards me. "You told your sister?" She asks me softly.

"You're going to marry Nevio?" Lucio asks her, "today? Because he won you in a poker game?" I think my sister is trying to check if I have kidnapped her or not.

"I did *not* kidnap her, force her, or in any other way harm her. Her brother arranged this. We don't know why but it is obviously serious so we will do as we are told, Lucia. Like go get a dress and flowers!" She rolls her eyes and Dalila laughs. Her smile is gorgeous. Even like this, in all of her not-so-morning-glory, she's stunning, and I can't take my eyes off her.

My sister taps away on her phone, leaning against the counter, occasionally looking over at me and Dalila as if she might be hallucinating and just wants to double check.

"I have nothing to change into." Dalila whispers, turning her back to my sister, her cheeks flushed with a pink blush.

"I'm sure I have something." The thought of her in my clothes has me growing hard against my pants. Fuck. Not now.

Flashbacks of last night have me heating up, and I'd rather *not* have those thoughts in front of my baby sister. I take her back to my bedroom and lay a white shirt on the bed for her.

"That should be good until Lucia gets a dress." Her blushed cheeks get redder and she nods. If I don't leave her to shower, I'll ruin my wedding night on my wedding morning. I back out of the room and go make sure my sister has understood the assignment.

"A messenger will be around with some dresses for 'me' to try on in about an hour, and I arranged for Cousin Leon to bring me some flowers. I lied through my teeth and said they were for a friend, so we get whatever he sends. Anything else?" She quips with a slanted smile. She can't believe this anymore than I can.

"No, thank you for helping me." I say as my driver comes in with my tuxedo he's collected. "I think I can manage the rest."

"The fact that you think you can manage Dalila Vece tells me you can't manage shit, but okay? When can I spill the tea?" She folds her arms and glares at me with a wicked grin.

"Later, after it's done." I say, "I mean it Lucia, this isn't some funny joke or latest gossip. Her brother hinted that they're in trouble. I promised I'd keep her safe and do this."

My sister looks disappointed, but I know she understands when I say trouble — we do not go looking for it.

"Fine, you guys always have all the fun." She sighs, "I swear to god, if my *other* brother doesn't have a real wedding and make me maid of honor, I'll be pissed. I've been robbed of my of sibling duty."

She's a brat, but at least she was a helpful brat today.

"I promise you can be God Mother when we make gorgeous babies, okay?" I say and she laughs, holding her belly. Her nose wrinkles, and I can tell she finds that amusing.

"Nevio, you couldn't keep a plastic houseplant alive. Please don't have babies." She snorts with more laughter, and I'm not sure if I am offended or impressed she knows me so well. Being the eldest son, an heir, is my responsibility, even if I am not taking my father's place. At one point or another I'll have to be a father — I sure as shit plan to be a good one when I do.

"Also, you can't see her in the dress. That is bad luck. Go get ready in the pool house. I will help Dalila, then disappear."

Lucia, like me, likes traditions.

They keep an order about things — and should not be disrespected. Before I can say another word, she adds, "My driver will get her where she needs to be, *and* if I am with her, I can't be tempted to tell anyone your dirty little secret." She's right.

"Fine," I growl, frustrated because I wanted to see Dalila in my shirt more than I wanted to see her in a dress. "But do not fuck this up. I like her. You forgot rings."

"You don't like anyone. You barely tolerate us." She frowns, poking fun at my antisocial nature. "And I don't forget things."

"I like you, somedays." I say, "Please Lucia, can you just not mess this up for me?" My sister stops joking, gives me a genuine smile, and nods.

"I won't," she says. "You deserve at least one lucky break in life."

I deserve more than that, but this one thing will do.

Chapter Seven

DALILA

When I get out of the shower, Lucia is sitting on the bed, surrounded by white dresses and a bouquet. "Short notice, so we have to just roll with what we have." She says to me like this is all somehow normal, that a secret wedding isn't a big deal. I stand there wrapped in a fluffy grey towel that smells like Nevio, and glance around, looking for him. "I sent him to the pool house. We don't want any bad luck, thanks."

"He won me in a card game. I think his luck is good." I say and walk over to the frills, bows and taffeta. None of them look like anything I'd choose for myself or wear. I'm a little disappointed that my wedding gown is going to be whatever fits on the day. "Thank you for doing this." I say, even though there's a heavy feeling in my chest.

"I did it for Nevio," she says, "don't hurt him, Dalila." Her eyes meet mine, and it's a plea, not a threat. I wasn't planning to hurt him. He's been soft and kind in all this. I wish my brothers had spoken to me though — warned me there was trouble. But if Mas asked him to care for me, there is a good reason for that. I trust my brother. Even when I hate him, I trust him.

I guess, to be honest, if he had warned me this was going to happen, I probably would have snuck out and avoided it somehow.

"I won't." I reply as she hands me a dress.

"Let's see you in these." I take a long look at the odd creation in my hand. "One of them will work."

"Not this one." I pull a face and hand it back. "There are a lot of bows on there."

Lucia laughs at me and tosses the dress over her shoulder. Digging through the dresses, she holds up a few that I am not interested in trying on at all.

"This is not awful." She says, holding up a short white dress that will hug every lump and bump of my body, but at least there are no bows or puffs. It's pretty — even though it's not a dress I imagined getting married in. I take it from her and go into the dressing room to change.

I don't like being naked in front of anyone, never mind someone I barely know. Lucia is younger than me, and not someone I was allowed to hang around. She is a 'wild child', according to my father. I think she is normal. What he considers wild is just growing up. And I have been held prisoner to his standards all my life.

The difference is, she has a mom. I think I would have had a different life if my mother had lived. Wiggling myself into the dress, I struggle against the feeling of it suffocating me. When I spin to face the full-length mirror, I don't know what to think.

I don't look like me — but me would never marry Nevio, in a dress his sister chose. I have to forget myself right now and remember that I don't get a choice. This is reality now. "Oh, wow." Lucia's voice gives me a fright and I spin around to where she's standing in the doorway. "My brother is going to love that." She walks around me.

"It's snug." I am uncomfortable showing so much of myself.

"It's hot," she says, "and we are racing the clock, remember? It's that or the bows and the frills."

I accept defeat and realize I only have sneakers here. That's going to be a sexy look.

"I don't have shoes here." I say and look down at the running shoes on the floor.

"Shit," Lucia says, "What size are you?" She asks me.

"A five," I say, "it's fine. I'll just make it work with my sneakers."

"You are not a 'runaway bride'" She shakes her head, "no, here I'm a five and a half, but these will do." She kicks off her black Manolo's and puts my high-top sneakers on her feet.

Oh well.

"Wait." She says, stopping me. Riffling in her purse, she pulls out a coin and slips it in the shoe. "We don't have all the borrowed and blue stuff, but I have *the sixpence for your shoe*. Tradition is important." I swallow a lump in my throat.

"Thank you." I mutter suddenly, more sentimental than I should be. "My shoes are borrowed."

I always wanted to wear my mother's pendant as my something old — and imagined my father giving me his blue pocket hanky as I got teary-eyed. This is nothing like I imagined, but Nevio is not the worst thing that could have happened to me.

She hands me a hairbrush and her make-up bag. "Sorry, I don't know what's in there, but I'm sure you can find enough to make yourself feel more bride-like."

I take it from her and look inside. Selecting the soft pink lip gloss and the black mascara, waterproof, as if I am going to be bawling my eyes out, I do my makeup.

Her skin tone is almost similar to mine, similar enough that when I dab her concealer under my eyes, it looks like it belongs to me.

"My driver will take you, and Nevio is going to wait there." Lucia is different from what I imagined her to be. She always seemed so bratty — I never expected her to be kind.

"This is very overwhelming," I say, sitting on the bed, looking down at my feet. The coin under my foot getting warm and moving slightly when I wiggle my toes in the shoes that are just too big for me. "I think I need to call my brother." I say, turning to look at my dead cell phone. I don't have a charger, and never thought to ask Nevio when he was here earlier.

"Your brother is the one who arranged all of this, isn't he?" Lucia asks, picking up her handbag and getting ready to leave.

"Yes."

"Then trust him, he might even be there, at the church. Come on, we have to get going." She walks towards the door and I jump up. "My brother will absolutely kill me if I get you to your own wedding late."

Chapter Eight

NEVIO

The tuxedo fits snug against my body, the high collar shirt hiding at least most of my birthmark. When I lean my head forward, my thick shoulder length hair falls into my face, covering the rest of it. I've never been able to change my hair, because at this length it serves a purpose. It hides me, my markings, my sins, my defects. I lift my head up again and stare at my reflection in the mirror.

Brushing my fingers through my hair, I push it back out of my face. I turn my cheek so that the red mark is clearly visible in the reflection.

Dalila didn't react the way I thought she would when she saw the full mark running over my shoulder and down my chest. When she traced the contour with her delicate, warm fingers, I didn't know whether to push her away or pull her closer.

Right now, though, all I want to do is pull her closer.

I can't believe I am marrying her today. Now. In the next hour.

I'm fully dressed, ready to leave, but just taking a moment to gather my thoughts and calm the weird nervous sensation drifting in my stomach. I'm getting married. Something I never thought I would have in this life.

Love, marriage, a wife - it's not made for men like me.

But now that I suddenly have this chance, I want to prove to the entire world that they've been wrong about me. I have a heart. I can love.

I will prove it.

I turn away from the mirror and that monstrous reflection. Grabbing my phone, I shake my head and clench my jaw.

I hope Dalila can see through my skin, into my heart.

I hope she can, one day, see me.

I walk from the pool house towards my car parked in the driveway. Glancing up towards the bedroom window, I see shadows moving inside the house. The girls are still in there getting ready. They still have time. The church is close. But I want to get there early to make sure it's safe.

The car bleeps twice as it unlocks and I pull the door open, sliding into the driver's seat. I press the ignition button and it purrs to life beneath me.

The drive to the church is quick and uneventful. I don't know why I feel as though someone is going to come leaping from every corner - to steal away my bride.

I park right by the entrance, a quick getaway if we need it, even though it also makes it obvious that I'm here. I'm choosing my battles today, based on the very limited information I have about this situation.

Usually, when I go to war with a man, I know what I'm there for. I know what I'm dealing with. Right now, I feel as though I'm in the dark about everything.

But darkness comforts me. It makes me feel alive and safe.

Within minutes of arriving, a second car pulls up and parks next to mine. I know who it is right away, so I stand leaning against my car waiting for Masaccio to climb out and tell me what the hell is going on.

"Nevio." He says my name as he slams his car door closed and his feet crunch on the gravel of the parking lot.

I nod. Watching. Waiting.

"I just wanted to make sure you two were going to go through with it. I know Dalila might try to pull something and make a run for it. I'm sure she's pissed."

I don't like to speak, not to anyone. But I have questions.

"She will be here." I say bluntly.

"I hope you're right." His brows at knotted at the sound of my voice. He's never heard me utter a word before. But today he doesn't taunt me or react to my sudden vocal freedom.

"What is going on?"

He shrugs and sighs, then runs his hand through his hair and leans his back against his own car. I fold my arms across my chest, waiting. I won't ask again. He heard me clearly enough.

"It's complicated. And I can't tell you much at the moment. But Nevio, Delila is in danger if you let her out of your sight. Once this marriage is completed - it makes it safer for her - but it not entirely. Do you think you'd be able to keep her in your house, out of the public eye, until we can resolve this? Until everything settles."

"Until what settles?"

"I'm sorry, man. I really can't tell you more than that. Will you keep her safe?"

"Yes."

"Does she hate me? For what I did?" there is a shift in his expression when he asks this. His eyes fill with a desperation, a deep fear, that she will never forgive him.

I stare at him for a long moment, then shake my head.

"She'll understand when you explain it to her."

His jaw clenches as she swallows hard.

Down the street, I spot my sister's car, driving towards us. "That's Dalila arriving." I lift my chin to gesture towards the approaching vehicle.

"I have to go," Masaccio says quickly, almost panicked.

"Not staying?" I tilt my head.

"No. Take care of my little sister." He says with an intense glare at me.

I glare back, not saying anything.

Lucia's driver pulls into the parking lot of the church and Mas ducks into his car, slamming the door behind himself, safely hidden behind the thick, bulletproof tinted glass.

I turn towards the girls, eager to see Dalia in her dress. But it's Lucia who climbs out first.

"What are you doing? You can't see her yet. I told you - it's bad luck. Get into the church and wait with the priest, you moron." She pushes at me, trying to get to me move up the church steps towards the massive wooden double doors.

"Wait." I say, trying to get my sisters to calm down. "Please give this to Dalila."

I hand her the box with a beautiful diamond bracelet I had made specially for her, a rushed order that cost triple what it should have, but I don't care.

Lucia takes it from me. "Okay, I'll give it to her. Now go away."

A low chuckle rumbles through me, and I resist the urge to turn and look towards Dalila again.

In a matter of moments - she will be mine.

Chapter Nine

DALILA

Lucia's driver pulls into a parking space outside the beautiful old church building with its massive hard carved wooden doorways and quaint iron vine balustrades leading up either side of the white stone steps.

My heart is pounding in my chest when I see Mas talking to Nevio. He came. My brother came. He will explain everything. Maybe he will tell me this was all some crazy joke. Maybe I don't have to get married and I can go back home.

"I told you your brother would be here." Lucia says.

I don't reply. I'm too lost in thought, staring at the men talking.

A weird pang of anxiety twists in my stomach when I think about leaving Nevio. I've only known him - properly for a few hours. But the thought of leaving him makes me feel weird.

Why? I don't owe him anything. I don't have feelings for him -

I take a deep breath as the kiss flashes through my mind.

Then his lips, traveling over my body, the way he touched my skin, his tongue.

Perhaps, just maybe, you can know someone deeply in a few hours. Perhaps, just maybe, all of this was meant to happen, and the universe just put me in the right place for a reason.

I force a smile onto my face, ready to accept my fate, but then when I look out the window I see Mas getting back into his car.

"Wait, no, where is my brother going?"

"Oh. I don't know. Maybe he forgot something?" She pulls her mouth tight, knowing that isn't true.

I lean towards the door to grab the handle and pull it open. Lucia moves faster and grabs my hand, pushing it away. "Don't. You can't let Nevio see you." She says in horror.

"I have to talk to my brother." I retort. Why does no one understand this? I don't know what's going on. I'm about to marry a man I'm not in love with. And no one has told me why.

But it's too late, anyway. Mas is already driving away. His heavily tinted windows hiding him from my eyes.

I blink back tears. What did he say to Nevio? What did they talk about?

Nevio is walking towards our car. He leans down to open the door and Lucia screams. "What is wrong with everyone? Do you want bad luck forever?" She opens the door and climbs out, closing it behind herself and standing in front of it to block Nevio's access.

Lucia scolds Nevio. They have a brief conversation, and he hands her something before she sends him into the church to wait.

My eyes follow him. He is massive, a beast of a man with broad shoulders that pull tight against his tuxedo. His high collar shirt is hiding some, but not all, of his red mark. As he walks up the church steps, I watch him pulling his hair over the side of his face. A habit I have seen him do it so many times since yesterday.

It's strange, but since last night, since that first time that I really looked at him. I mean at *him*, not at his devil mark — I can't unsee how beautiful he is. I can't not notice it now that I've noticed it.

He disappears into the church, and I bite my lip nervously.

So why was Mas here and why didn't he just take two minutes to say something to me?

Lucia pulls the car door open. She has a massive smile on her face. At least someone is happy.

"Come on, you can get out now."

I climb out of the car, and she hands me a small velvet box. "It's from my brother."

I open the lid and stare down at the most beautiful bracelet glittering in the light.

Lucia glances over the lid. "Oh, wow." She lifts it out of the box. "Give me your hand. It's something new, so we have almost all of it." Clipping it onto my wrist, she smiles as she admires it. "It's gorgeous. Ok, let's go. It's time." She does a little wiggle, like a happy dance. I stop myself from rolling my eyes because all of this seems so fucking ridiculous. But another glance down at the bracelet makes me smile.

He is trying to make this special and I really appreciate that.

I take a deep breath, pulling the tight white dress down slightly so my ass cheeks don't hang out in the back.

Lucia pushes a bunch of flowers into my hands and stands on her tiptoes to clip a veil in my hair, then pulls it over my face.

I close my eyes for a moment while she fusses about.

It's going to be ok, Lila. It's going to be ok. This isn't what you ever pictured when you thought of getting married one day - but - it's - going - to - be - ok. I force each word into my brain. Making myself calm down, pushing the anger, confusion and worry away.

When I open my eyes again, I feel better.

I really am good and numbing myself.

"Ok, let me go into the church, then wait five seconds and come in." Lucia says, then takes my hand and pulls me to the top step. With one last glance at me, she disappears into the church.

I count in my head.

One.

Two.

Three.

Take a deep breath.

Four.

Open your eyes.

I step into the church. The change in light from the bright natural light outside to the darker, orange candle lit glow of this massive space makes me blink a few times, waiting for my eyes to adjust so that I can see more clearly. The veil isn't helping either.

I trust my feet for the first few seconds and walk.

Then I see Nevio, standing at the altar, his hands clasped in front of him, his shoulders back. His face is stone serious as he watches me, and I can't help but wonder what he's thinking.

His eyes bore into me like a blade, piercing through the veil into my soul.

I chew at my lip nervously as I keep walking towards him.

Stopping in front of him, I hear the priest clear his throat. It echoes in the very empty, massive space. Bouncing off the high ceilings and along the stained glass windows.

When he speaks, I jump a little.

"Are we ready?" he says, his voice old and scratchy. I glance towards him, his wrinkled face and grey hair — but he has a warm smile.

"Ready." I say.

Nevio steps towards me and slowly lifts my veil.

Now I can see his face more clearly and I find it impossible to look away from him. It's as though he has me tied to his gaze. Inescapable blue eyes. Piercing and bright.

We exchange vows and I'm on autopilot. I keep fiddling with the flowers in my hands. My fingers tugging at the leaves around the base of their stems.

Nevio is still staring.

"I now pronounce you man and wife. You may kiss your bride."

Suddenly, his lips spread into a wide smile. Dimples form in his cheeks, his eyes seem to glow, and he steps towards me, wraps his arm around my waist and pulls me right up against him.

He doesn't dip me, by he lifts me off my feet as he kisses me.

That kiss.

That kiss brings back all the sensations I experienced beneath his touch last night.

I hear Lucia laughing in the background. Nevio sets me down on the ground again.

"Let's go home." He smiles.

I have so many questions about why my brother was here, but now doesn't seem to be the right time. I turn to look at Lucia, and she quickly brushes a tear from her eyes. Her smile is making her face glow, and it makes me smile in response.

Nevio leads me out of the church after we've signed all the documents. We say a quick goodbye to Lucia, who announces that she is going to be telling *everyone*. It's sweet how excited she is for her brother. I think they're really close. It lets me glimpse a side of Nevio no one else has.

On the way home, I finally pluck up the courage to ask questions.

"My brother — what did he say?"

"Let's just get home first." Nevio says, his eyes on the rearview, watching, alert and ready for anything.

I scrunch my brows together. "Is something going on?"

"Let's just get home, Dalila." He says forcefully and I feel myself getting angry.

I clamp my mouth shut and stare out of the window in silence.

Inside the house, I toss the flowers onto the kitchen counter.

"We're home. Tell me what the hell is going on. What did my brother say? Why didn't he stay and talk to me?"

Nevio walks over to me, reaching out to me. He runs his hands down my arms. A gentle gesture. "Your brother said that there is still danger, even now that we are married, and that you are to stay in my house for the moment. You may not go outside."

"Excuse me?" so even after pawning me off to some random guy, my brothers are still trying to control me? Still trying to stop me from living my life?

"He wants you safe, Dalila."

"Bullshit. If he wants me safe, he can tell me himself. He should have stayed to speak to me. Anything. He didn't even have one minute for me. He expects me to just go along with all of this without explaining a fucking thing."

Suddenly, the anger is boiling inside me and I can't control it.

I push Nevio's hands off me, wanting to leave, wanting to go home.

"Dalila, stop this at once."

"Who the fuck are you to tell me what to do? Everyone wants to control me like I'm some toy. Some doll."

"I am your husband, and I only want you to be safe." He did not just say that!

"Then tell me what's going on? Husband! Why is everyone keeping secrets from me?" I snap, heated. My cheeks burning from anger.

"I can't." He says, his eyes narrowing, frustration creeping onto his face.

"Then leave me the fuck alone until you can." I push him away, my hands against his solid chest. He doesn't even budge. So, I step around him and storm up to the bedroom. I need to be alone.

Chapter Ten

NEVIO

Dalila stomps off, her feet heavy against the stairs as she tries to get her anger out with each step she takes. I close my eyes, my heart feeling heavy. This is not the evening I had hoped for when we came back from the church.

I don't know if I am supposed to give her space or grab her in my arms and hold her close.

I don't know how the fuck to handle a woman. I've never had to deal with this before.

Why can't she see that I'm just trying to do what is best for her to keep her safe, like her brother asked?

I can't tell her what's going on because I don't fucking know.

I pick up a book, laying on the counter near me, and fling it across the room in anger. It hits a standing light and both smash to the floor.

"Fuck." I shout.

I head into the living room where I have a bar built into the wall and pour myself a whisky, downing it, letting it burn all the way down my throat, searing against my skin and distracting me for an infinitesimal moment.

I'll give her a little bit of time to cool down, then I'll go in and talk to her. I need to explain that I don't know enough yet. But I'll find out. I'll do anything for her. She is my wife now - my life - my everything. And I will do anything to make her happy. To keep her safe.

All I wanted on my wedding night was to lie in bed with her and feel her skin, explore her body, claim her properly as my own. I showed patience last night. Tonight I want to push my cock inside her and own her.

My cock stirs at the thought.

I try to ignore it.

Pulling my jacket off, I toss it onto the sofa nearby and pour another drink. My thoughts are running wild now. Just one momentary image of her beautiful, naked body, and now I'm losing control. She is my wife and I need to claim her.

I pull the top few buttons of my shirt loose as I pace up and down the living room. Glancing at my watch, I realize she's been upstairs for an hour already. I can't take it anymore. I've given her enough time and I have to make this right.

I have to make her mine.

She's so angry with me, but I'm not the bad guy. Not this time. I climb the stairs two at a time, my long legs making it look easy. I push the closed bedroom door open and step inside.

"Dalila."

The bed is empty. My heart leaps in fear. Where the fuck is she? Did she leave? How can I be so stupid?

But then I see the blanket on the sofa near the window in my room. It's moving as she breathes, tucked safely under it. I shake my head. I already made it clear last night that she will be sharing my bed. Why would she think I'd let her sleep on the couch? Especially now that we are married.

I walk over to her, looking down at her - the way her waist dips in as she lies on her side, her legs curled up against her chest. I take the corner of the blanket and drag it off her, revealing her body, inch my inch.

She's taken off the dress, and she's wearing my shirt. The one I wanted to see her in.

My cock pulses.

I pull the blanket further off her body so that I can see everything. The way the shirt has drifted up over her back and her gorgeous ass is on display. I lean down and run my hand over her thigh, inside her leg.

Stop. What are you doing? She's not even awake. This isn't how you wanted it to be.

My mind and my body fight wildly. Both wanting to overthrow the other as my cock throbs and begs to my thrust into her.

I step away from her, closing my eyes to shut out the beautiful image of her soft skin and perfect curves.

Stop.

Pick her up.

Take her to bed.

Let her rest.

I lean down and gently wrap my arms beneath her, lifting her slowly. She stirs, muttering in her sleep. Still angry by the sounds of it.

I carry her over to our bed and place her gently beneath the covers. Then I strip down and climb in next to her, pulling her against my stomach as I hold her tightly. She can't leave. She can't escape. I made a promise to keep her safe.

Tomorrow I will have to make her understand everything. I will have to find out what is really going on as well. I can't keep her safe unless I know what I'm protecting her from. Her brothers need to tell me something.

I fall asleep with my cock hard and throbbing against her. Dreams of her body infect my thoughts and I keep waking up through the night, fighting against myself, understanding a whole new level of what self-control really means.

Chapter Eleven

DALILA

It's dark when I feel myself waking up, trapped somewhere between dreams and the real world, after midnight. Immediately, my body begins to thrum and pulse with desire. I shift in my sleepy state and feel him against me, his body wrapped over mine, my back pressed into his chest.

And I can feel his cock.

I arch my back and press my ass against it, letting the dreams drift through my mind as I move slowly, playing with him, enjoying the sensation of his cock pressed between my ass cheeks.

I hear a low growl from behind me and it pulls me further awake.

Oh fuck.

I'm not on the couch anymore. And I'm not dreaming.

His cock is rock hard and pushing into me.

I try to wiggle a little away from him, but his arms lock tighter around me.

"You shouldn't have done that." A low vibration as his voice runs through me. My body is tingling, my pussy is drenched at the feel of him.

But I'm angry. I won't give in to this.

Fuck. Don't. Don't give in to this.

My body betrays me as I try to wiggle away from him again, but I arch my back even further, to rub my pussy over his cock.

Oh my fuck, it feels so good.

No.

Don't give in to this.

He doesn't even respect you enough to tell you what is going on.

Don't give in to him.

His hand grips tight against my waist, then brushes over my skin, gripping my hip as he pushes against me with his cock.

His breathing is heavy, deep, and filled with need.

"Stop that." I demand in the darkness. My voice coming out far less commanding that I had hoped, and even as I tell him to stop my fingers are digging into his arm, my body twisting against him still, begging him to fuck me.

"I can't." He warns me. "You should never have done that."

I try to turn around, to say no, to tell him he can't have me, but he rolls onto me, pushing my face against the pillow, his chest against my back as he pins me to the bed.

"Nevio." I say, a whisper of a breath.

I gasp as he pulls my legs apart and his hand wraps around my throat from behind. He lifts my face and his lips trace over the side of my neck, causing goosebumps to spread across my skin. I spread my legs wide.

I don't want this.

I desperately want this.

His hand is between my legs, his fingers brushing over my pussy, and electric bolts are shooting through me.

He dips his fingers inside me, and I push against him, trying to drag him deeper into me.

"Stop." I whisper again, but it's useless.

"No." He growls against my ear as his finger slips out of me and I cry out in horror, wanting the feeling back.

But then his cock presses against my pussy and I can't think.

I can't think about anything.

I can only feel.

He slowly thrusts forward. Pushing himself inside me.

I feel my pussy spread wider than it's ever before.

Pain shoots through me and I whimper softly.

"Does it hurt, baby girl?" He asks, but he doesn't wait for my answer. He keeps sliding his massive cock into me.

I can't answer, anyway.

Pain is turning to pleasure, and the pleasure is almost unbearable.

I lift my ass towards him, wanting more. Wanting everything.

He pushes his cock all the way into me, buried inside me. He stops moving, letting me adjust, letting my pussy relax. I can feel his cock twitching and throbbing.

"I'm OK," I whisper and he growls low and deep, an intense sound of need that rumbles against my back. He fucks me, slowly, moving in and out of me rhythmically. He reaches his hand around the front of my body and cups his fingers around my pussy as his cock penetrates me, he moves his fingers in circles over my clit.

He is fucking me harder and faster.

Pushing deeper, thrusting forward repeatedly.

The sensation is more than I can bear, and I am moaning and rocking myself against his hand.

His breath is hot against my neck when my legs shake uncontrollably.

I feel so overwhelmed by physical sensation and emotion that I scream when the orgasm washes over me in waves after wave as his cock continues to thrust inside me.

My pussy clamps over him and I hear him moan - then his cock grows even bigger and I feel him exploding inside me.

When it's over, he rolls off me, pulling me along with him so that I stay wrapped in his arms.

He whispers into my ear. "You are made of the same things angels are made from."

I want to be angry. I want to push him away, but I'm too tired.

I close my eyes and drift off to sleep in his arms, feeling safe and warm and like I am the most beautiful girl in the world in his eyes.

In the morning, the soft light pulls me awake before him.

I blink against it, trying to remember where I am and process everything that happened.

My hand is resting on the pillow near my head and the diamond ring catches the light, making me swallow hard.

I'm married.

My brother wouldn't talk to me.

I had sex for the first time last night.

It was so fucking amazing, but - I can't let that fool me into thinking that what they are doing is fair.

I deserve to know what is going on and why they expect me to stay trapped inside this house with Nevio.

His breathing tells me he is still fast asleep.

I grin, remembering last night, but then quickly push the thought away.

I slide myself out from under his arm and tiptoe out of the room.

I need to think.

Everything has happened so fast. My name has even changed, and I don't think my mind has caught up with any of it.

Dalila Armano.

Wife of Nevio Armano.

Does he have a second name?

Something you'd think you'd know about the man you married and lost your virginity to.

I make my way down the stairway to the kitchen. The house is quiet. It's earlier than I thought it was. The light outside is softer than I thought it was, too.

I flick the kitchen light on, and the brightness stings my eyes.

I wonder over to the coffee machine and flick that on too. Standing on my tiptoes, I grab a mug from the kitchen cupboard. But I can't reach.

It's so obvious he lives here alone, with no female in sight. He's so tall and everything is out of reach for me.

I wiggle onto the kitchen counter, my knees on the edge, as I hold into the cupboard handle for balance. I grab a mug and place it on the counter next to me, then lower my hands to the counter to get down.

"What are you doing?" His voice comes from behind me and I freeze with fright.

My naked ass pointed right at the kitchen door. My cheeks flush bright pink when I remember what he did to me last night.

"That's a beautiful view, but can I help you down before you hurt yourself?" He chuckles.

I wiggle off the counter and bash his hand away when I feel it on me.

"I'm perfectly capable of doing things on my own." I huff, annoyed and angry and not about to let him distract me with that amazing body of his again.

"Ok, ok." He steps away from me with his hands raise, his brows knotted. "Are you alright? Did you sleep ok? Does anything - uh - hurt - from last night."

"Humph." I snort at him, lifting my nose in the air like a proper brat. "Tell me when you're done in the kitchen and I'll come make my coffee then." I snap, then push past him and leave him standing alone.

Chapter Twelve

NEVIO

I wake up, and Dalila is already up. I panic as my eyes open and I don't feel her next to me. I promised to keep her safe.

Sitting up, the first place I check is the sofa. In case she crawled back there last night, but it's empty.

I hear a loud sound from the kitchen downstairs. Ok. She's still here.

Pushing the blankets off me, I stretch, grab a pair of sweatpants and pull them on before making my way downstairs.

I walk into the kitchen and it's a sight I could look at all day.

She is on the kitchen counter, her hands resting in front of her, her naked ass pointed right at me, her bright pink pussy on display.

A sly grin touches my lips and I imagine myself grabbing her hips and fucking her exactly where she is. My cock throbs.

"What are you doing?"

I say, not too loud because I don't want to give her a fright. She already looks like she might fall. I guess I should shift things in the kitchen around so that she can reach the daily things more easily.

She glances behind herself and I notice how pink her cheeks are.

"That's a beautiful view, but can I help you down before you hurt yourself?"

I walk towards her, ready to lift her in my arms, but as soon as I reach out to help her she brushes my hands away with a sour expression.

She's still angry.

Last night didn't change that.

"I'm perfectly capable of doing things on my own." Her eyes dance up and down my body, taking me in. She looks like she wants more of what I did to her in the dark hours of this morning. But she also looks like she wants to skin me alive.

"Ok, ok." I wonder if I hurt her last night? Maybe I was too rough. I know it was her first time. I wanted to be more gentle, but I couldn't. She was just so - prefect.

"Are you alright? Did you sleep ok? Does anything - uh - hurt - from last night."

She gives me the brattiest little glare I've ever seen in my life and says, "Tell me when you're done in the kitchen and I'll come make my coffee then." Then she pushes around me and leaves.

I stare after her in shock.

She really is going to be a challenge for me.

I don't even know how to respond to that.

Should I be hurt? Should I be angry?

The only thing I know for sure is that I want to repair whatever has damaged the connection we seemed to have when she first arrived here.

I sigh as I pull another coffee cup from the cupboard and start making both of us a cappuccino.

She's still angry that her brother didn't take the time to talk to her at the wedding. And I think she thinks I'm hiding something from her.

She's put up some pretty intense walls around herself now and I need to figure out how to break them down.

Carrying the coffee through the house, I finally find her outside on the patio. It's cold out, but she's wrapped in a thick blanket and has her legs pulled up against her chest. I put the coffee down on the table next to her and then pull the outdoor overhead heater nearer and flick it on. The red glow bakes down towards her.

She doesn't even turn to look at me.

"Dalila?" I say.

"Please leave me alone. If you won't tell me what's going on, just leave me alone."

"I don't know what's going on. I only know what your brother told me."

"Whatever. I'm tired of being a pawn in this game and not understanding any of it." She sighs, still keeping her eyes away from me.

My heart aches to pull her close and hold her in my arms.

I step closer, and she turns to glare at me. Fire in her bright green eyes, warning me not to test her. I know I could overpower her easily. I could pull her onto my lap and hold her and she wouldn't stand a chance against me — but I don't want to make her angrier —

or push her further from me. I have to move with caution.

The only thing I can think of doing is contacting her brother to push him for information.

I turn away from her and leave her in peace on the patio, watching across the garden as small, soft snowflakes dance in the air. The morning light that was here only a few moments ago has faded behind a grey sky.

Her brother is going to have to tell me something. I won't let him create tension between my wife and me.

I walk into my bedroom, feeling the chill of the air against my skin. I grab one of my turtleneck sweaters and pull it on, shivering.

I can't believe how quickly the cold creeps in.

I pick up my phone and dial Masaccio.

"Mas, it's Nevio."

"Nevio. Is my sister ok?" he sounds worried.

"She's fine, but pissed off and wants answers." Hell has no fury like an Italian girl scorned.

"I don't know what to tell you —"

"Not good enough. I want answers, too."

I hear a heavy sigh drifting through the line.

"Meet me. In an hour. I'll explain everything I know but not over the phone. It's too risky. The Archers Bar on Bree Street in town. One hour."

"I'll be there."

Town is busy despite the cold weather and thin layer of ice on the pavements. It's the holiday season and people want to shop. There are smells of cinnamon latte and chai tea drifting in the air. And a Santa on every other corner.

I push the door of the bar open and a wall of hot air slams against my body, along with the assault of holiday music. I don't know why they insist on playing this music in all public spaces. I get it. It's Christmas, but can we listen to something else?

I close the door behind me and feel claustrophobic. I Don't want to take off my black trench coat, but it's so fucking hot in here. Why do they always pump the heating so high? It's unnecessary. People are walking around the bar in tee-shirts, playing pool, drinking cold beers. The temperature contrast between indoors and outdoors is astounding.

I shrug the trench coat off and drape it over the back of my chair, sitting facing the door, still overheating in the turtleneck jersey, but not a fuck am I going to take that off and have everyone staring at me in a matter of minutes.

Self-consciously, I run my hand across my cheek, down my neck, then pull the turtleneck higher to cover my devil's mark.

The barman walks over to where I'm sitting.

"What are you having?"

I look around the place. It's not even lunch yet.

Whatever.

"Whisky, on the rocks."

He nods and walks away.

The door chimes, a soft jingle of a bell as it opens, and I lift my eyes to see who's coming inside.

It's her brother.

I watch his face as he walks into the wall of heat. His nose scrunches up in annoyance and as he walks towards me, he's already shrugging his coat off his shoulders.

"Nevio." He says, hanging it over the back of the chair next to me and then pulling it out so he can sit down.

"Masaccio." I reply.

"Quite festive out there, isn't it?" He chuckles, dry and unenthusiastic.

I stay quiet.

The barman puts my whisky down in front of me and looks towards Mas without a word.

"Same."

Once he's settled and has his drink, I get straight to the point.

"You need to tell me what is going on, otherwise I can't protect her."

"I know, man." He sighs. "The problem is that I don't know the entire story. I only know what my dad bothered to tell me and that was enough to let me know I had to make a different plan to the one he had." He's gone against his father, which is a red flag.

"Tell me what you know." I push. Getting annoyed and beginning to understand why Dalila is so angry at everyone.

"That night of the poker game. Well, earlier that day —" The barman arrives with his drink and he pauses, takes a sip, and waits for the guy to leave again. "Earlier that day, my father called me into a meeting alone. He told me that someone had information about him and the family. He had to make some kind of deal."

He pulls his mouth tight and shakes his head. "That deal was exchanging my sister for the safety of the family."

"Exchanging her by giving her to who?"

"One of our rivals. Lenny Malone."

"Are you fucking serious?" Even I can't believe that.

That man is a psychopath. He is doesn't have a single bone of empathy or softness in his body. He would kill a man for blinking at him wrong and now Mas is telling me that her father was going to hand his own daughter over to that monster. And he isn't even an alley. He's a rival.

Now, you must understand something.

I am called a shadow, a monster, a villain - and I've earned it - but Lenny Malone - he would have skinned Dalila for fun. I don't understand what her father was thinking.

"It doesn't make sense." I shake my head.

"I know. But that's why I did what I did on poker night. If she was married off to someone else before Malone got his hands on her - well - fuck man. I had no choice."

"I agree. You had no choice. Is this why our fathers were not there on poker night?"

"Yes, all of them were out — concluding this deal." He nods, then picks up his whisky and drains the glass.

"And what happens now? Where is Malone?"

"I don't know where he is, or my father at the moment, but I know one thing. Malone is pissed off and looking for revenge for the dishonored deal. That's why you need to keep her locked up, out of the public eye. It's just too risky."

"And that's all you know? There isn't anything else you are keeping from me?"

"Nothing else, man. Please tell Lila I'm trying to find dad. I'm trying to fix this."

Chapter Thirteen

DALILA

I watch through the massive upstairs windows as Nevio climbs into his car, the collar of his long black trench coat pulled up over his face, hiding him from the world.

I'm angry, sulking, fuming, wanting to lash out even though there is no one to lash out at.

I still do not know what's going on and now Nevio is leaving me here, not telling me where he's off to - and he told me I wasn't allowed to step out of the house. Not even into the garden.

What the fuck is going on with everyone and why am I a prisoner here?

His car pulls out of the long driveway and I watch it as he drives into the street and speeds away.

I shake my head.

I guess all of them have forgotten who I am.

All of my brothers, my father, did they really think I was just going to do as I was told?

I wait until I am one hundred percent sure that Nevio is gone and not coming back for some random reason.

Then I spin away from the window and start grabbing my things. My phone, my jacket, my sneakers.

I have to get out of here. I want to go home. I'm not sure if that is the best idea — but at least if I go home, I can confront Mas and make him tell me what this is all about.

He can't avoid me forever.

Nevio trusts me - which makes me feel bad. The guards were not put on high alert to watch me, but rather to watch the perimeter of the property for possible intruders. I guess he assumes I am staying inside.

He s mistaken.

I bite my lip as I walk down the stairs towards the front door.

Wrapped up in my hand is the key to the security gate along the footpath leading out of the garden. It's a quiet and less obvious route to take as opposed to trying to leave through the main gate.

I wait for the security guard to walk past and continue his routine around the garden.

I've been watching them all morning, so I am confident I know how much time I have to make it to the gate.

Counting in my head, I make a run for it, straight for the bushes along the edge of the walkway. I stay low and keep moving.

Fifteen.

Sixteen.

Seventeen.

Duck down.

Stay quiet.

I wait for the footsteps of the next security guard to move past me, then I look up over the bushes that are hiding me.

And go.

Now I'm just running flat out, feeling the burn in my lungs as the cold air smacks into them. I reach the gate and fumble with the key for a second because my fingers are so frozen.

It's fine. I'll warm up on the walk to town.

It would have been great to take a car, but there is no way I could have made it out of here with a car.

I'll call an Uber when I'm far enough away from the house.

I click the gate closed behind myself then start on foot down the road, staying near the tree line, ducking low whenever a car comes past in case it's Nevio.

It feels so good to be out in the open, away from the restrictions and the rules and people not telling me anything.

I grin as I jog, wanting to get to town faster.

But the grin fades really quickly when I see men following me on foot.

Surely the guards didn't see me? If they did, they would have shouted or come after me in a car?

I glance behind me. Three of them, moving fast.

Wearing black gear and army boots. They are security — but they don't work for Nevio. The uniform is wrong.

Fuck.

I run a little faster. I'm not cold anymore. My blood is pulsing though me at a decent pace and warming me up to where I want to take my jacket off. But I don't have time for that.

Glancing left and right along the street, all I see are trees.

I'm going to have to go into them. It's risky because then no one will see me along the road in order to maybe help me - but I have to because I can't outrun these guys or hide from them out in the open.

I dart left, the wet ground mulches beneath my feet as I push through the trees into the forest. I can feel the dampness soaking into my clothing.

I'm dressed for town, not for a hike. And being wet and cold in the weather is a deathtrap in itself.

Don't stop moving until you find somewhere good to hide.

I just keep talking to myself in my mind. It's the best way to stay calm in situations like this.

I hear the men shouting behind me, somewhere in the trees, the sound bouncing in too many directions, echoing through the forest and making it difficult to know what direction they are coming from.

I have to hide. My legs are so cold they barely want to move anymore.

I can feel tears of panic and fear pressing against my eyes. No. Now is not the time to break down. Hide. Think. Move.

Ahead of me, I spot a massive rock outcrop and a fallen tree. I run towards it. There is a drop on the other side of the rock, down a steep slope that looks treacherous to be trying to walk on in this wetness.

I take a deep breath and step over the fallen tree.

My sneaker slips and I skid a few feet down the slope, grabbing onto some spiked shrubs to stop myself.

My hands are cut and bleeding.

I pull myself up into a small ditch on the muddy earth and press my body into it.

Holding my breath, I count.

Counting keeps me calm. It steadies my lungs; it slows my heart rate.

I hear the men, close, talking loudly, not afraid of being seen or heard like I am.

"Where did that little bitch go?"

"Malone is going to kill us if we miss this chance to get her."

"Well, what the fuck are we supposed to do? This place is a shit show. It's fucking cold."

"Do I look like I fucking care about your discomfort? Find her or it'll be your skin he wants instead of hers."

"It's a lot of effort to go through just so he can kill her."

My heart is beating so loudly that I'm sure they will hear it.

The tears are streaming down my cheeks, leaving wet lines that the wind is biting at.

"Hey, over here, there are some skid marks. I think she went this way."

Fuck.

They are even closer. They must have seen where I fell.

"There - you can see where she went—"

"Do you think she fell all the way down the slope?"

"No. The marks in the soil stop—there—"

"Fuck. We have to go down there."

"Get moving."

I don't know whether to hold my ground or run.

I try to move, and the ground slides away beneath me. If I move wrong, I will slide all the way down the slope and it's a pretty rocky, steep fall. I won't survive it. But what's worse?

Lenny Malone or falling off the side of a cliff face?

Honestly, the cliff face is the kinder option.

I've heard the stories about Malone. I've heard my brothers talking about him.

How is he involved in this? Why is he after me?

I hear heavy thuds as one man slides down the side, using his knife to spear into the wet earth as a grip. I look around from where I'm hiding and it's the worst timing because I look directly into his face. His dark eyes lock with mine and he stabs his blade into the soil to shift himself lower, closer to me.

"She's fucking here. That stupid bitch is making me fucking filthy."

"Get her. Don't let her get away."

Chapter Fourteen

NEVIO

All the way home from the bar, I am thinking about Lenny Malone and what kind of monstrous things he would do to Dalila if he got his hands on her.

It's eating me alive and making my skin crawl just to think about it.

At least I can explain a little more to her about what is going on.

Perhaps with this new information she will be more open to talking to me again and we can work on our relationship again.

It frustrates me she is pushing me away. That first night - I knew it was too good to be true. Too intimate, she was too open and tender and eager.

"Fuck." I mutter, remembering her begging me to make love to her.

I pull into the driveway at home and there seems to be some kind of issue.

One guard runs up to my window before the car has even come to a stop.

"She's gone."

"What?" I shout. "Impossible."

"We were just about to get on the phone and tell you - she's gone. We watched over the security footage and she made a run for it about forty minutes ago."

"What the fuck?" I shout, anger burning from my lips.

I grab my phone and scroll through my apps, looking for a very specific one.

The app that links me to the diamond bracelet on her wrist.

It has a tracking device in it.

The signal tracker spins for a moment, trying to locate her. I grit my teeth in nervous tension, thick anxiety bubbling in the pit of my stomach as I wait.

There.

"She's not even that far from here. Did you say she left forty minutes ago?"

"Yes, sir."

"In a car?" My mind is racing. Her location is off to the side of the road, and I can picture her having rolled a car, now trapped inside it.

"No, sir — she left on foot."

"What?" I mutter.

Fear grips me as I rev the car into action. I head toward the tracker. It's only about ten minutes down the road by car.

I park on the side of the road by the tree line and start jogging towards her.

In no time at all, I hear voices. Men.

I duck low. I know the drill. Watch. Gather information. Don't rush into a situation that you haven't read yet. It's a guaranteed way to get yourself killed.

I can't see Dalila anywhere.

The three men are dressed in security wear. The typical black army style uniforms, guns strapped to their legs, rough looking faces. Scared and dangerous.

"Where is that little bitch go?"

"Malone is going to kill us if we miss this chance to get her."

"Well, what the fuck are we supposed to do. This place is a shit show. It's fucking cold."

"Do I look like I fucking care about your discomfort. Find her or it'll be your skin he wants instead of hers."

"It's a lot of effort to go through just so he can kill her."

Fuck. They are Malone's men, which is the worst-case scenario.

If they find her before I do —

No. I can't let that happen.

"Hey, over here, there are some skid marks, I think she went this way."

Fuck.

They are looking over the edge of some sort of slope. It looks pretty steep.

"There - you can see where she went—"

"Do you think she fell all the way down the slope?"

"No. The marks in the soil stop—there—"

"Fuck. We have to go down there."

"Get moving."

The man moves down the slope. The knife he has in his hand makes me uneasy.

I have to move too. I have to stop them.

I pull my knife from the ankle strap.

"She's fucking here. That stupid bitch is making me fucking filthy."

"Get her. Don't let her get away."

They are so focused on what the guy is doing over the slope that they don't see or hear me coming up from behind them.

I grab one man, and his throat is slit before he knows what's happening.

From down the slope, I hear struggling and Dalila screams. A sound that churns my insides.

He has his hands on her.

The man I've just killed slumps down and I catch him, lowering him quietly. The second man catches sight of my movement from the corner of his eye and turns towards me with a surprised gasp.

He's too late, though.

I swing my arm as I turn to face him, and the blade of my knife pierces through the base of his chin, erupting from the top of his skull.

Sick, gurgling wet sounds drip from his mouth as he tries to scream.

I drop his body over the slope, no longer worried about being stealthy. I want to send the third man a message.

"What the fuck?" His voice carries up to me.

I lean over the slope, looking down at him with my gun aimed at his face. He has Dalila in his grip, but he looks unstable. His footing is slipping.

"Dalila, baby girl, hold into something." I say calmly.

Then I fire two shots into his shoulder. I don't want to kill him from here and have him fall while still holding her.

His scream is deep and guttural as it pushes through the cold forest air.

He lets her go to grip his injured shoulder.

As soon as he does, I put a single bullet between his eyes.

Dalila screams when blood sprays across her face from the man who was hunting her.

He slips away, falling down the slope, moving in some kind of slow motion as his body tumbles and slides.

I holster my gun.

"Were there more of them?" I ask her as I slowly make my way down the slope.

"Dalila, were there more men?"

She looks up at me, her lips tinged blue from the cold and her hands shaking as they grip against the branches of a small tree. She shakes her head.

She looks terrified, bewildered, like a small animal trapped in a hunter's snare.

I reach her and pull her into my arms, digging my heels into the dirt to grip.

I hold her against my chest and kiss her face.

"It's ok, baby girl. It's ok, I'll get you home." I whisper against her cheek, my warm breath heating her skin. She is ice cold. Shivering and wet.

We move slowly and carefully as I help her back up the slope.

A small cry falls from her lips when she sees the body of the man at the top. "Don't look." I say, pulling her face against my chest. "Come on, the car isn't far."

I know Malone is waiting for his men to return. He will find out what happened.

It's only a matter of time before he comes again, this time with more men and more anger.

In the car I pump the heating even though it is a short drive.

I am holding her against my side as we drive along the quiet road towards home.

She hasn't spoken, and I haven't pushed her.

She needs to feel safe first. Then I will ask her what is going on. Why she left and what happened with those men?

For now, I just want to hold her, let her know I'm here for her.

Chapter Fifteen

DALILA

Sitting in the car with the heater blasting over my legs, my mind recovers from the survival panic it has been clinging to for the past hour.

The relief I felt when I saw Nevio looking over that slope, down towards me, I can't even describe it.

I wanted to cry out to him, call his name, but my lips wouldn't move.

Fear and cold had sunken too deep into my skin at that point.

And only now - on the way home - is it releasing its grip from me.

Nevio has his arm wrapped around my shoulder. I am almost lying on his lap while we drive. I close my eyes and count to ten, soothing my heart, easing away the fear.

I hear the familiar sound of the house gate opening and the crunch of gravel beneath the tire that tells me we are home.

I sit up, looking out of the window and my heart pulls tight when I feel this strange sense of relief and safety — thinking — I'm home.

My mind is happy to think of Nevio's place as *home*.

My door opens and Nevio is standing there with his hand outreached. He pulls me out of the car and lifts me into his arms to cradle me against his chest.

I lean my face against his warm jersey, not wanting to meet the eyes of the security guards all staring in wonder at me.

I hear the front door close behind us. Nevio carries me up the stairs to our bedroom, and through to the bathroom. He sits me down on the edge of the bath, then leans over it to turn on the hot water.

I watch him as he pours salts and into the rushing water. Steams fills the bathroom and fog the mirror.

"Get undressed." He whispers.

I look down at my clothes, covered in mud and dirt.

I don't move.

"Come on, baby girl." He pulls me to my feet and while I stand there feeling bewildered, he peels my clothes off. Layer by layer until I am standing there shivering, staring up at him with wide eyes, wondering why he just killed three men for me.

"Dalila?" He asks, looking down at me. "Are you ok?"

I reach up and touch his cheek. His skin is warm. My hands are like ice against him.

He doesn't flinch, though. He reaches up and threads his fingers through mine, pressing my icy fingers against his cheek.

I lift myself onto my tiptoes and kiss him.

I don't know why I did it.

I just wanted to feel him.

He pulls my naked body up against him. His hand is resting on my lower back as he returns the kiss. Slow and deep. Our lips moving together as though we are dancing.

Then he stops.

"You're shivering. Come on." He lifts me in his arms and into the bath, lowering me slowly as the hot water stings my skin.

I sink into the aromatic steam and let the heat eases my stiff body.

Nevio kneels next to the bath. Picking up a sponge, he strokes it over me.

He works and with care.

I close my eyes and take a few deep breaths, finally able to accept that I am safe now.

I should never have tried to leave.

"I'm sorry." I mutter in the quiet silence that is drifting between us.

I open my eyes and look into his. So blue they look like rare diamonds.

"It's ok, Dalila. I know there is a lot going on, but — please —"

"I won't do it again." I interrupt him, knowing he is going to ask that of me.

He nods, still rubbing the sponge over my skin.

"Why did you try to leave?"

"I hate being kept in the dark. I hate being controlled." I say, feeling guilty for making him come and rescue me and having to kill those men.

"I went out this morning to meet with your brother." He says.

"You did?" I sit up a little.

"I wanted to get some answers for you. I know you've been struggling without knowing what's going on, and I don't blame you."

"What did he say?" I ask eagerly.

"Your father sold you off to one of his rivals." He says, his voice tight with anger.

"Lenny Malone?" I say, putting the pieces together. "Why would he ever do that? That man is the darkest type of monster known to man."

Nevio nods, his eyes drifting over my body.

"Your father told your brother that the family was in some kind of trouble and he had to make a deal with Malone to keep them safe. He sold you - you were the deal."

My chest feels so tight it's getting harder to breathe. I sit up in the bath and press my hand against my heart.

"My father sold me to that man - " I whisper, trying to process what it means. "But Mas — "

"Mas bet you in that poker game on purpose. He thought that if he could drunkenly 'lose' you, then at least you would end up married and out of Malone's reach."

I nod, but the tears are streaming down my cheeks. I understand why my brother did what he did - it was the only thing he could think to do in that situation - but the idea of my father trading me off like I was stock - it makes me sick inside.

How can someone do that to their own family?

He could have asked me. He could have told me what was going on and I might have gone willingly. But to do it behind my back as though I meant nothing. And he still hasn't spoken to me since then. No explanation, no words of comfort -

"Where is my father?" I snap, feeling heated anger flood me and replace the self-pity.

"No one knows. He is in hiding. Or - or Malone found him." Nevio shrugs.

I sink back into the water, needing the warm embrace again. My thoughts are racing.

"I want to speak to him. I need to know why. I need to know what was so worth it for him to sell me to a man that he knew would kill me. My life. He traded something for his own daughter's life." My words choke in the back of my throat and I can't speak anymore.

Suddenly I am sobbing, heart wrenching, painful sobs of misery that flood out of me in loud cries.

Nevio hesitates, unsure what to do, but then he leans into the water, lifts me back into his arms and pulls me onto his lap, dripping wet, soaking his clothes.

He wraps a warm, soft white towel around me and rocks me back and forth as he sits on the bathroom floor.

I cry until I can't cry anymore. Nevio doesn't stop comforting me.

Finally, when my tears are no longer falling, he stands up, lifting me with him, and carries me to the bedroom.

He finds comfortable clothing for me to wear and dresses me, his hands brushing against my naked skin, his eyes wandering over me the entire time he is moving and my heart beginning to pulse with a new fever.

I grab his wrist.

He pauses, looking concerned or confused.

Then, without warning, I slam my lips against his and start pulling his wet clothes off.

Layer by layer, I strip him down because all I want to do is feel his skin against mine. I want the touch of his body. Nothing between us.

He lifts me and throws me onto the bed when we are both naked again.

He grabs the blankets and wraps them over both of us, lying his body over mine, his hands beginning to explore me.

Chapter Sixteen

NEVIO

I am doing my best to treat her with respect, to comfort her, to take care of her despite this untamed urge I have at the sheer sight of her naked skin.

Now is not the time, though. She doesn't need me to be putting that kind of pressure on her after everything she's been through today - and after what she just found out about her father.

She doesn't know yet.

She doesn't know that I love her.

And the more she pushes me away, the harder I fall.

I will wait for eternity for her to love me back.

Until then, I will hold her. I will take care of her.

I will keep her safe - if she continues to let me.

When her crying softens and stops, I stand up off the bathroom floor and lift her in my arms. The towel falls away from her back and I can't help running my hands over her skin - hot from the bath.

In the bedroom, she stands still as I try to find something warm for her to wear.

The towel drops from her body, and my eyes roam over her.

Fuck.

She is way too fucking gorgeous.

My cock stirs, beginning to throb and press against my pants.

I clear my throat, trying to clear my mind of the images of her - but it's impossible. She is all I see.

As I pull the hoodie over her head, my hands brush against her skin. I slow down, letting my fingertips play over her curves.

I shouldn't do this.

I feel like I'm taking advantage of her.

I wish she wanted me as much as I wanted her. Every second around her is agony. Agony of loving someone who isn't interested in you.

She looks up at me, standing there in nothing but the oversized hoodie.

Her eyes meet mine, and I am drawing in green pools of glittering light.

My heart thunders like a storm in my chest.

Then her lips are on mine, and her hands are pulling at my clothes.

For a second, I think I'm dreaming, but my body is all too real against hers.

She strips me down, layer by layer. I drift my hands beneath the hoodies, really caressing her now. Touching her, taking her in.

Then I lift her arms over her head and pull it off her again.

Naked, our bodies against each other, neither of us notices the cold anymore.

I throw her onto the bed, my thoughts becoming more intense, darker, and flooded with desire at each passing moment.

Beneath the blankets, my hands push between her perfect thighs and she lets out a gasp when I press my fingers into her pussy.

She is breathing heavily, her chest moving against me when I move my fingers in and out of her. She is rocking her hips in time to my movement and the little sounds she is making are causing my cock to become so hard it's aching.

I pull her thighs apart, rolling onto her. I force her legs wide with my hips, lifting her legs against her chest. Folding her in half beneath me.

She moans as I brush my cock over her spread open pussy.

Wide and waiting for me to slide inside her.

She reaches up and wraps her hands around the back of my neck, pulling me towards her, a silent way of begging me to thrust my cock into her and fuck her.

I lean close to her ear.

"Never leave me again." I growl against her cheek.

Her eyes are wide.

"If you leave me again, I will have to punish you and I don't want to punish you, baby girl."

She whimpers and rocks her hips upwards, pressing her pussy against my cock. The tip of my cock sinks inside her and I growl again, a low, deep rumble of pleasure.

I press deeper, feeling my cock push her pussy open as I glide deeper and deeper.

She lets out a heavy breath against my skin; her nails digging into my shoulders.

I push so deep into her; I feel as though I might rip her apart.

Then I pull out again, slowly.

I pause, waiting. Her pussy throbs over my cock.

I thrust forward and slam inside her.

She screams and grips me tighter.

I fuck her, rhythmic movements that are making her moan and writhe with pleasure.

She feels so fucking good trapped beneath my body like this.

My little girl, my baby, my wife.

She is mine, and I will never let her go.

"You belong to me, Dalila. DO you understand?"

She nods.

"No other man will ever touch you. You are mine." I growl, a threat and a warning.

The truth.

I will tear anyone who touches her apart. I will pull them to pieces and make them suffer.

She is mine.

Dalila is shaking beneath me, her body shuddering with each thrust into her pussy. My cock can feel how tight her pussy is getting as she nears her orgasm.

I grab her chin and pull her face towards mine.

"Look at me when you come. I want to watch you."

Her lips part open, and warm air escapes her mouth.

Her breathing is even faster now, her pupils dilated.

Then I feel it.

Her pussy clamps over me, sucking my cock deeper into her.

Waves of pleasure rush through her and her eyes stay locked with mine as she comes all over my cock.

I slam into her one more time and feel myself exploding inside her.

We lie in bed for a long time, not saying anything, just wrapped up in each other's arms. I want to know what she is thinking, but I'm scared to ask.

I'm scared that she only kissed me because she was in shock from what happened. I am scared that if I speak, she will push me away again.

So I just hold her, feeling the pulse of her heart as it beats against my chest.

Letting my fingers trace over the bones of her spine, shaped beneath her skin.

Feeling her warmth and hearing her breathing.

After a long time, I feel her body shake.

I move her so that I can see her face, lifting it from where she was laying against my chest.

Tears are running quietly down her cheeks.

I sit up and pull her into my arms.

"I'm so sorry for what happened." I whisper.

"My dad — I just — I don't understand." She cries.

"I will find out what happened, Dalila. I will find out for you. You deserve to know." I stroke my fingers through her blonde hair.

She nods, then snuggles into my arms and closes her eyes.

Chapter Seventeen

DALILA

I have never met such a gentle and caring man before.

My brothers, growing up with them, they took care of me — but they were rough, controlling, bossy, bullies even.

I know they loved me, and I know they would always take care of me, but this is so different from that.

Nevio is tender.

He is attentive, doing sweet thoughtful things.

I have never met such a gentleman before and I never, in my life, in a million years would have said that Nevio would be a man like that.

It's like he has these two sides to him, and I am the only one in the entire world who gets to see this side of him.

An image flashes through my mind.

His eyes, how they looked when he stood at the top of the slope, just before he threw the dead man's body over the edge, and just before he shot and killed the third man.

That cold, empty, deadly stare.

That is the Nevio everyone else knows.

When I look into his eyes, I don't see any of that. I know he would never be that person towards me.

For me, yes.

But not towards me.

Nevio has gone into town to collect a few things. I am sitting in the living room, playing on my phone, watching series - not doing anything.

The weather is still freezing today and while it isn't snowing, it's still a good time to be snuggled indoors.

I smile, picturing myself snuggled against him.

No, what am I doing? I can't be falling for him. Can I?

I giggle at myself.

I think I am falling for him.

It might be a really stupid thing to do, but how can I help it?

I don't even see his birthmark when I look at him anymore. I see his deep blue eyes, his grin, the dimples that form on his cheek. The dark shadow of stubble across his jaw. The shape of his jaw and his neck, where it curves towards his broad shoulders.

I giggle again. Dammit. I am falling for him.

He makes me feel so - loved.

Like he loves me for me. Not for what he wants me to be. Just for me.

I haven't ever felt that before.

"Ehem."

I jump at the sudden sound and spin in my chair, turning towards it.

"Who are you?" I stammer. I thought I was alone this entire time. How long was this guy standing there? Who the fuck is he?

I am tense and slowly moving, ready to leap to my feet.

"Calm down, pretty little thing."

He drops onto the sofa next to me.

What the fuck.

"I'm Nevio's brother." He says, throwing me a charming smile.

He holds out his hand towards me. "Damion." He says.

I take his hand and instead of shaking mine; he runs his thumb over the back of my hand.

"Mm. So soft."

I yank my hand back, feeling instant ick.

Oh, he's gorgeous. He has Nevio's eyes, and a similar shape to his jaw. His mouth is different, but he has the same dimples.

I stare at him, though, feeling grossed out because his entire attitude is kind of slimy and forward.

I shift away from him, further to the other side of the sofa.

He notices and cocks his head to the side.

"Where are you going, little bird?" He snarls and leans over, grabbing my thigh and pulling me across the sofa towards him.

He locks me in place as he shifts his body over mine. HIs eyes lock with mine and I sneer at him. "Get the fuck off me right now." I hiss.

"I don't see why he gets you. You should have been mine. He's so fucking ugly I don't even know how you look at him."

His fingers are digging into me, and his words infuriate me. No one should ever call Nevio ugly in front of me.

I let my leg up to my chest and kick out hard, catching him in the ribs.

He huffs as the air is slammed from his lungs.

I spin and try to crawl away, but he grabs me and drags me back to him.

Now he is lying on top of me on the couch and I'm getting loud.

"Get the fuck off me." I scream.

"I just want a little taste." He laughs as his hand wraps around my face and pulls me towards him. His lips are inches from mine.

Out of nowhere, he gets lifted off me and begins flying across the room.

Nevio is standing over the couch, looking down at me. My eyes are wide and bright with tears.

"Are you ok?"

I nod.

He turns towards his brother, who has picked himself up off the floor.

His voice is low and terrifying as he marches towards him with sinister intent.

"Who the fuck do you think you are coming into my house and laying your hands on my wife?" He thunders as he shoves his brother backwards.

Damion staggers and only just stays on his feet by gripping the edge of a bookcase.

"Grow the fuck up, Nevio. You don't deserve a girl like that. Look at your fucking face. Look at her. She's fucking gorgeous — and you — you look like something that should have died the moment it was born."

Nevio swings his arm, and his fist connects with his brother's jaw.

He doesn't stop there, though. His brother is caught off guard, and one hit might have been enough to shake him, but Nevio is blind with rage. He keeps hitting.

His fists slamming against his brother's face over and over again.

I stand up and run towards them, screaming at Nevio to stop.

He pauses when he hears me, his fist hovering above Damion's face. Blood covering Damion's skin and Nevio's knuckles.

"You'll kill him. Please, Nevio, stop." I beg.

Damion laughs, a wet low sound, coated with blood.

"She's wants me, man. She'll trade me for your ugly fucking skin any day."

Nevio pulls his arm back again, ready to punch, but I grab his elbow.

"He's not worth it." I whisper.

Nevio looks towards me with pain in his eyes.

I can tell that his brother's taunts are something he has had to endure his entire life. The cold cruelty of his brother's words stabbing into him.

I reach out and touch his cheek.

Nevio's eyes soften as they gaze into mine.

He stands up, leaving his brother laying on the floor, coughing.

"You can let yourself out, asshole." Nevio says, without turning to look at him.

All the commotion has drawn the attention of the guards from outside.

Two of them are standing at the doorway.

"You can make sure he leaves — as soon as he can stand." Nevio says.

The guards nod and walk towards Damion.

Nevio pulls me into his arms and I grab his hand, looking at his knuckles, already turning a bright shade of blue.

"Let's get some ice." I say, pulling him towards the kitchen.

We both step past Damion without glancing in his direction.

What an asshole his brother is.

I shudder to think what would have happened if Nevio hadn't arrived home when he did.

I push Nevio against the kitchen counter, taking control of the situation, wanting to take care of him the way he has taken care of me more than once.

Gently holding his hand in mine, I press a bag of frozen vegetables against his knuckles. He doesn't even wince, and when I look up at him to see if he's ok he has a slight grin on his face.

"What's so funny?" I ask curiously.

"Nothing."

"Then what are you smiling at?"

"You." His smile grows wider and drops the frozen veggies as he pulls me into his arms to kiss me.

Chapter Eighteen

NEVIO

I am standing in the kitchen with Dalila in my arms, our lips locked, her heart beating against my body.

"Nevio." My brother's voice calls out to me.

I lift my head towards the sound. Not letting go of Dalila.

"What?" I snap.

He is standing in the kitchen doorway. The two guards are right behind him, ready to grab him if he tries anything again.

"I'm sorry, man." He mutters, sounding sorry for himself.

"You're sorry you got your ass handed to you." I snark.

"Yeah man, I'm sorry about that too. But really, Nevio. I'm sorry. I don't know what I was thinking. She's —" He clears his throat. "Your wife is beautiful."

"You're speaking about her as though she isn't right here in the room with us."

He nods, looking down at the floor.

"Dalila, I'm sorry." Damion says. It's the first time I've ever heard him being that polite to a woman. He rarely treats them with respect.

Dalila looks from me to him. I shrug. It's her choice if she wants to accept his apology or not.

"Ok." she says, after a while and my brother's shoulder relaxes a little. Then he lifts his chin, trying to regain some of his dignity. His face is still smeared with blood from the fight.

"I'll head out. I just came to meet - I came to - I'll let myself out."

"Good idea." I say coolly.

I wait, listening for the sound of the front door closing. Then I let out a heavy breath. My fucking brother is an endless source of stress for me.

"He has always been my father's favorite." I mutter, more to myself that to Dalila.

"Why? He's such an asshole." She says with full sincerity.

I laugh.

I can't help it.

It's so funny because more accurate words have not been spoken more plainly.

"He really is an asshole." I laugh deeper. Then Dalila is laughing, too.

It feels good to just stand here in the kitchen laughing with someone.

Someone beautiful. Someone with a soft and caring heart. Someone who sees through my obvious flaws, who doesn't look at me as though I am a monster - someone he seems to see *me*.

"Thank you." I say after a pause. Brushing my hand across her cheek to tuck a stray curl of hair behind her ear.

"For what?" She asks as she stares up into my eyes, warming my soul.

"For stopping me. From doing something stupid. He really is an asshole, but I was pretty close to breaking his jaw and that would have caused a lot of issues between my father and me." I grin.

"He wouldn't have looked a right idiot with his jaw wired shut. And - even better - he wouldn't have been able to speak properly for a good long time." She tries to reason with me playfully.

"So, you're saying I should have broken his jaw?"

"I'm saying he *might* have deserved it." She grins.

"I know he did. Even though he is my brother, and I am almost fully certain he wouldn't have hurt you, just what he did was enough to deserve a broken jaw. I'm so sorry he touched you like that."

"I'm ok, Nevio." She says as she nuzzles her face against my chest, wrapping her arms tighter around my back.

"You're perfect, Lila." I whisper, with my lips pressed against the top of her head, breathing in the scent of her hair.

At dinner that night, Dalila sits right next to me. It's the first time she's done this. She usually sits in the chair opposite, basically as far away from me as she can.

She reaches out beneath the table and touches my leg, drawing my attention to her even though she already has all of it.

"What's for dinner?"

"I think you should wait and see — the chef should bring it out any second now." I grin.

She scrunches her nose and sniffs the air carefully.

"It smells like—"

The chef walks in and places a glass dish of seared salmon with crispy baby potatoes and lemon slices. Then another plate of caramelized vegetable, cut long and thin and finally, corn on the cob coated in butter and salt.

She stares at all of it with her jaw dropped open.

"It's—" she stammers over her words.

"It's your favorite meal." I finish for her.

"But—how did you know—everything, even the corn, how did you—"

I grin as she stares at me in disbelief.

"I asked your brother, baby girl. I wanted to surprise you."

She grins, ear to ear, her entire face shining.

"That's so sweet of you." Her hand is on my thigh again as I dish up for her. I expect her to pick up her knife and her fork, but she doesn't. She just picks up the fork and starts eating, her other hand still on my thigh, burning heated fire into my skin, sending shivers of delight through my body.

After dinner we are sitting in the living room, her wrapped in my arms, as we watch some cooking show that she seems to enjoy. I'm not paying too much attention because I can't seem to drag my eyes off her.

Every time she glances at me she asks, 'are you watching?' And I say I am, even though I'm not.

She is too beautiful. She is too perfect.

Do I even deserve something this special?

My phone vibrates against the coffee table, and she leans forward to pick it up for me. She hands it to me then snuggles back into my arm.

I slide to unlock the screen and navigate to my notifications.

My heart stops.

"It's a message from your father, Dalila." I say, not wanting to ruin our peaceful evening.

She sits up and stares at me with wide eyes.

"What did he say?"

"He wants to meet up and talk."

Chapter Nineteen

DALILA

"He wants to talk?" My throat feels tight and my mouth is dry.

"Yes. Do you want to?" Nevio asks me, letting me decide.

"We kind of have to. We need to know what is going on. I have — I want to ask him so many questions — but, it won't change what he did." I sigh, a heavy ache building in my heart at the thought of my father.

"I will arrange for them to come to the house tomorrow." Nevio says, running his hand over my back reassuringly. "If you change your mind, we can cancel. And don't worry about any of it, baby girl, no matter what happens - I will always be here for you. I will always take care of you. I won't let anyone hurt you, Lila."

I like it when he calls me Lila.

I like it more when he says I'm his baby girl.

I nod at his words and snuggle back against him. "I'll worry about that tomorrow. Right now, I'm - happy." I say, feeling Nevio tense beneath me. He feels rigid for a moment, then his hand drifts up my back, caressing me.

"You're happy?" he asks, tentative.

"I'm happy." I whisper, smiling, not knowing how to explain how or why I feel that way if he asks me, but knowing that for the first time in a very long time, I really feel genuinely happy.

I keep glancing at my watch.

The diamond bracelet glittering on the same wrist whenever I move my arm.

I can't stop pacing, up and down, up and down, nervous to see my father.

"When are they coming?" I ask for the hundredth time.

"They are about five minutes away." Nevio has endless patience. I have no idea how he hasn't screamed at me to shut the hell up yet because I am at the point where I'm annoying myself, so I *must* be annoying him too.

I continue to pace until I hear the door chime - security letting us know our guests have arrived.

I sit in the living room, tense and awkward, with my father sitting opposite me and my brother's on either side of him. Only Masaccio and Red have come with.

"Rufino, Mas, Vincenzo - thank you for coming." Nevio greets them as he sits down next to me, wrapping his hand over my thigh, not caring about the look my father throws in his direction. I thread my fingers through his and press his hand tighter against my leg.

I take a deep breath. Rufino looks pissed off, and I wonder if they all had a fight on the way here or something. Mas is sitting tense and quiet.

"Red? Are you ok?" I ask. He nods, his bright red hair and the shadow of fire colored stubble growing across his jaw is the reason we all call him red. He's a good-looking guy. But of course, that didn't stop my other brothers from tearing into him for having red hair while we were growing up.

It's been a long time since they taunted him, though. Now that he is a head taller than even my oldest brother, his height, and bulk are an imposing threat to anyone who wants to mock him. The jagged scar above his eye adding to his Viking sort of look.

Red nods. "I'm good." He says, throwing an angry look at my father.

Oh. I see. He's angry at my father.

My dad clears his throat. "Lila, I wanted to come and talk to you."

I turn my eyes towards him, and my fighters tighten over Nevio's.

He squeezes my thigh, a wordless gesture to let me know he's right here with me. My heart constricts. I smile, because he makes me feel safe.

"Talk then." I say with confidence that Nevio has given me.

"I came to explain why — what happened. You'll understand. I know you will." He is falling over his words, perhaps nervous, perhaps unsure where to start. I wait patiently.

"A few months ago, one of our allies turned into a rat. The fucker got caught for something and in exchange for not going to prison, instead of just serving his own fucking time like a man, he started spitting out names to the cops. My name. He gave the cops my name and a lengthy list of shit I have done - with evidence. None of my own rivals could help because they would be in just as much trouble as me if their names got mentioned."

I stare at my father, waiting to find out what this has to do with me and Lenny Malone.

He shifts in his seat.

"I was in a dangerous position because I was going to jail. I started asking around, looking for any way I could get out of it. That's when Malone approached me. We've never seen eye to eye. We've never gotten on or even done business together. But he said that he would make that fucking rat disappear if—"

He coughs, rubbing his hand across his throat.

"If I gave you to him."

I stare in total disbelief.

I don't think my father can hear the irony in his own words.

I stare until I can't hold back my anger for another second. "So, you made the deal. You gave me to Malone, the most monstrous man on the planet, so that you didn't have to go to jail?"

"Yes, sweetheart, you have to understand—"

I stand up, fuming. Fire flaring in my eyes are I shoot my anger towards him. "Oh, I *understand*. Do you want to know what I understand? I understand Malone would have killed me. Perhaps not right away, but he would have. It would have been painful and torturous." My father opens his mouth to interrupt me. "Shut up and listen. Don't say a word." I warn him. "I understand something else, dad. I understand you want to call your alley a rat for rolling over to the police to save his own ass from jail - yet you are a hypocrite. Because you rolled over to Malone to save *your own ass from jail*. You rolled over so badly that you were willing to sell your own daughter's *life*." I am shouting at him, losing my voice, losing control, shaking and furious.

Nevio stands up and pulls me into his arms, trying to calm my shaking body.

I push him away and turn back towards me, father. "What makes your life any better than your own child's? What kind of father sacrifices his own daughter to save himself some time in jail? Time you would have paid to have shortened. Time you would have spent in privacy, protected luxury. Not in the general prison population. I know how it works." The more I talk, the more I hate him for what he tried to do.

Tears are streaming down my face.

Was stands up, Red stands too, they both turn towards my father. Red grabs his arm and pulls him to his feet. "It's time to go," He says, his deep voice rumbling through the room.

"Dalila, I just - " My father tries to reason with me.

Mas shakes his head. "No, dad, it's time to go."

They pull him out of the room, and he walks with his shoulders slumped forward.

I stare after him and realize that he never saw the reality of the choice he made. He never said that he had also thrown someone one else under the bus - me.

He seems to only have just come to that understanding now as he slinks away from me, walking out of the house that my brother got me into.

I turn to look at Nevio, suddenly so grateful for him, so happy that he fought so hard in that poker game for me. I step close to him and he holds me tight against his body.

I lean my face into his chest, soaking up the warmth and feelings of security.

"I'm so happy it was you." I whisper, fighting fresh tears.

"Me too." He responds, stroking my back. "I thank God for it every day."

For the rest of the day, I walk around the house in a daze. Still angry, feeling lost, like someone has ripped the ground out from beneath my feet and I'm drifting in space.

My childhood, all the memories of my father, are flooding my thoughts.

I can't seem to see him in the same way I used to.

I used to look up to him. He was this giant, this unbreakable man who could do anything. He was strong and scary and commanding.

But now, after today, all I see is a weak man who will throw his own daughter to the wolves to save his own skin.

And even scarier than that is that he didn't even realize what he was doing. What choice he was making. He was so hellbent on survival that he only saw what he wanted to see.

How many times in my life have I thought he would die for me?

I sigh.

Why am I even letting these thoughts go on a loop like this? I need to shake this horrible feeling off. I need to let go.

"Come to bed, baby girl." Nevio says, pulling me from my mind. He reaches out and grabs my arm. "Come to bed," He says again, when I don't respond.

I nod. "That's probably a good idea." I say, feeling distracted.

Chapter Twenty

NEVIO

Dalila is struggling with deep emotional pain after finding out exactly what happened.

I don't blame her. Her father should be ashamed of himself. I can't believe he would do that to his own daughter, someone so pure, so sweet, so innocent. I can't believe any father would do that to their child.

"Come to bed." I say again, because she didn't seem to hear me.

"That's probably a good idea." She says, glancing up at me as though she has no idea who I am. Her eyes are drifting, lost in a storm out at sea.

I smile and wrap my fingers between hers. "I've made hot chocolate. It's on the bedside table." I say, pulling her up the stairs towards the bedroom. She follows me without talking. Her silence is heavy, and I feel my heart breaking for her.

I feel as though her entire view of who her father is has shifted, and she now has to process this new reality.

When she is dressed, she climbs into bed. I pull the blankets up over her body and tuck her in, leaving just her arms out.

Handing her the hot chocolate, I sit on the edge of the bed next to her.

She sips at to as I brush my fingers across her cheek.

"I don't think he stopped to think about the choice he was making." I say, trying to find some way to comfort her. "I don't think it was done out of - what I mean is - I think he loves you deeply, Lila. He was scared, and he made a really stupid mistake. Your brothers are furious with him. I can see it."

She looks up at me, her eyes narrowed as she listens.

A soft sigh falls from her lips, her breath drifts towards me, smelling like hot chocolate.

"I think I understand that - but - isn't that part of the problem. He never even stopped to think about me. I don't even think he saw me as his daughter when he made that choice. I was just a tool. A pawn to be used in his negotiation. Anything and everything was worth risking just to keep himself out of jail. And I saw what happened when his friend went to jail. He was there for six months before he paid his way out. And during those six months he had a private cell, with a tv and internet and good food. Visitors any time he wanted - " She sighs again.

"I don't really want to think about it anymore. It hurts too much."

I nod. "What can I do for you, then? How can I make you feel better, baby girl?"

She looks up at me again, her eyes sparkling with tears. "I hate the thought that someone who I thought loved me would do that to me. Do I not understand love? Has anyone ever loved me if my father can -" Her throat closes over her words and she wipes the back of her hand across her face.

I reach out and use the pad of my thumb to brush away her tears. Then I bring my thumb up to my lips, licking them off, tasting the salt from her body.

Her lips part as she watches me, her demeanor shifting. She runs her tongue over her lips, and I can see by the way she is looking at me she is no longer thinking about those things.

I pull the blankets off her and take the mug out of her hands.

I crawl onto the bed, kneeling over her.

"I would burn in the fire of a thousand suns to keep you safe." I whisper. "I want you to know what true love is, don't ever leave me."

Her eyes grow wider.

I push my hand beneath her hoodie. My hoodie. The one she keeps stealing from me to sleep in because she says it is the most comfortable.

"I love it when you don't wear panties." I growl, letting my fingers tease across her skin.

She reaches up and pulls my jersey over my head, leaving me topless above her.

Her fingers trace my birth mark, contouring the edges. This time I don't feel ashamed. I don't feel as though I need or want to hide from her.

Beneath her touch, I feel beautiful. It's in the way she looks at me. The expression in her eyes is warm and loving.

She looks at me as though she has love for me.

Does she just not know it yet? She's never told me she feels anything like that for me.

I lean down, pressing my lips against hers as I lay my body over hers.

I feel our heart beats sink, beating in time to a rhythm that only we know.

Her hands run over my back, slowly, drifting as though we have all the time in the world to explore each other.

She spreads her legs, and I tug my sweatpants down enough to free my cock.

There is no wild desperation, no tugging and pulling, no heavy breathing or skin glittering with sweat. There is just her and me.

She wraps her legs around my waist, and gently I push my cock inside her pussy.

We are staring into each other's eyes, neither looking away, neither saying a word.

I rock my hips back and forth as I watch her expression.

My cock thrusts in and out of her body, feeling the tightness, then pulling away and immediately wanting to push back inside her.

I don't let myself speed up, even when I desperately want to.

I don't let myself move faster or push deeper.

I can see it in her eyes — the way the slow tension is driving her so close to the edge and she doesn't understand how. She's never felt this before.

This is more than sex.

This is what it feels like to connect to someone's soul.

I've never felt it either, but I have wanted to — my entire life I have wanted to feel this way.

I reach up and hold her beautiful face in my hand. She rocks her hips up towards me, also moving, matching my rhythm.

I lean down and press my lips against hers and slip my tongue inside her mouth. Now I am fully penetrating her. My tongue. My cock. I am inside her, pushing deeper, pushing harder.

The feeling of kissing her while fucking her becomes too much to bear and soon my body is shaking against hers. She grips me tighter and her pussy locks over me.

The orgasm that pulses through her is the most intense one I've felt. I can barely move my cock she is gripping me so tightly. She tilts her head back and isn't breathing as her body convulses with pleasure.

I can't hold back.

My cock explodes in wave after wave as I shoot my pleasure into her.

She is everything.

She is my world.

My universe.

My life.

My love.

"I would burn in the fire of a thousand suns to keep you safe." I whisper to her for the second time, because I need her to know. I need her to know what it feels like to be loved.

Chapter Twenty-One

DALILA

I wake up in the morning in Nevio's embrace.

Sleepily, I open my eyes just a crack and reach up to wrap my hand around his bicep, tracing the curves and touching his skin.

Last night left me speechless. The way we connected. The way he moved with me. It was like he could read my mind. I never knew it could feel that incredible. The books I read - they were always heated, spicy, wild, dangerous - but that - that was something completely different and something I don't even know how to describe.

For the life of me.

I can't make my heart stop beating wildly every time I think of him.

Is this what love feels like?

He makes me feel seen. Like maybe I am the only person in the entire world he wants to see. He makes me feel heard and appreciated. He makes me feel beautiful, happy, safe.

It must be love.

I grin and close my eyes again. Outside the window I can see soft snow flakes drifting in a breeze. It's so warm and cozy inside here - I'll just snuggle for a little while longer before I get up.

I feel him moving, rolling, and pulling me with him.

He lets out a yawn and then buries his face in my hair.

"Morning, little cutie." He says, running his hands up and down my back as he stretches out his legs, trying to wake his muscles up.

"Morning." I smile, pressing against him.

Glancing over at the alarm clock on the side of his bed, my eyes shoot wide open.

I dozed off again and slept for another hour and a half.

"Is it coffee time?" he asks, looking down at me.

"Definitely." I agree.

We both climb out of bed and Nevio hands me a thick black dressing gown, fluffy like a blanket. He rolls the sleeves up for me because they are too long and then ties the cord around my waist, so I don't trip over everything.

"Cozy?"

"Very."

Down in the kitchen, sitting on the edge of the counter staring down at my woolies socks with panda bear faces on them, while Nevio makes the coffee, I am thinking about my father.

"You're very quiet." Nevio steps close to me and runs his hands over the outside of my thighs.

"Just thinking."

"About?"

"My dad."

He nods, listening, giving me a chance to say something if I want to without pushing me for information.

I sigh, then thread my fingers through his. "I might want to meet with him and ask him some questions. I think last night everything took me by surprise — finding out what he did — it shocked me, and I didn't actually say the things I wanted to say or ask him anything."

"What would you ask him if you could?"

"I want to understand what he was thinking. Maybe, I don't know, but maybe it will help me - it just hurts so much that he made that choice. Like he didn't care at all. It's not how I viewed him, you know. He's my dad. He's always been my *dad*. But now I can't see him the same way again and it's really bothering me."

"Your entire perspective has shifted?"

"Yes. Everything I thought I knew about him - it just doesn't match up in my head anymore."

"Do you really think that talking to him will help?"

"I hope it will. Because how else am I going to understand it?"

"In my life, I've come to realize that some things are not meant to be understood. Especially when dealing with other people's selfish choices. It's sometimes just better to let it go - but it doesn't mean you shouldn't at least try to understand first. But - if it doesn't turn out the way you want - just know that everything will still be ok."

I nod. He's right. I might never understand why my father did what he did - but I do need to talk to him.

Nevio makes the arrangements for me. I am going to meet my father at a coffee shop in town. Nevio is sending one of his guards with me as I've asked to go alone. I need to speak to my dad alone. Nevio is not happy about that part of it, but he agreed. I think he can see it in my eyes - how much I need to do this.

At eleven thirty Nevio is standing at the side of the car, holding the door open and looking down at me, sitting in the back.

"Keep your phone on you. Call me if anything happens. I'll be there in a matter of minutes." He keeps shifting from foot to foot as though he's nervous.

"Nev, it'll be ok. I'm just going straight there and straight back. My father also has his security at the coffee shop, so I'll be safe."

"Mm." He sighs, not convinced.

He leans down, grabbing my jaw in his hands and kissing me deeply.

"I'll see you in an hour." He says, setting a time limit on my outing.

I grin and nod. "An hour."

The car door closes and the driver heads towards town. My stomach is twisting nervously, dread building in the base of spine and tingling all the way up my neck.

Maybe I'm making a mistake. Maybe I don't need to know. What if I don't like the answers he gives me?

I chew on my bottom lip as we get closer and closer.

The sound of screeching tires makes me jump. My heart is slamming against my chest.

The window next to me explodes inward, sending glass glittering through the car. I pin my head away and feel it landing like snowflakes in my hair. Sharp, tiny shards of glass.

The driver is pulling the wheel left, but our tires aren't even on the ground anymore. His head slams into the roof of the car and blood explodes from his nose.

I scream. I can feel the air being forced from my lungs, but I can't hear anything.

My ears are ringing, a high-pitched tone that is constantly drowning out all other noises.

I don't know how long I am hanging upside down in the back seat, my hair spilling over my face as it reaches for the roof, blood running to my cheeks and making my head feel heavy and painful.

Hands reach through the window and grab at me. A massive knife slices across the safety belt and my body slumps forward. I reach my hands up to stop myself from falling onto the roof of the car, but someone already has me. Hands are pulling me out of the vehicle.

I can see the shattered glass everywhere, blood pooling from the side of the car where the driver is. I can't see him though.

The car is a wreck. A right off.

Still in someone's grasp, I try to reach forward for my cell phone, but I get yanked back, sending pain shooting through my neck. Then a heavy boot kicks my phone away.

Don't do that. I need to call him.

I need him to come and get me.

I want to go home.

"Get her in the van."

The ringing stops and noise assaults my ears. All at once.

Sirens, screaming, men shouting.

I am lifted and tossed into the back of a white delivery type van.

"No." I scream, not understand what is happening.

"Shut her up, for fuck's sakes."

I turn to look at the men talking. I don't know why I expected to see the uniforms of paramedics — but I see very familiar-looking security uniforms.

The same uniforms worn by the three men who chased me in the forest.

I can't breathe.

I can't scream.

Everything is spinning with thick panic coursing through me.

Malone's men have me.

It's not what I want to do, because my father always taught me not to show weakness, but tears are flooding down my cheeks. I can't stop them.

I can't hold back the idea that the only person who knew I was going to be out here today was my father.

Did he give me up again - did he sell me out a second time?

The thought churns in my mind as the van speeds away from the city towards a location outside of our territory. Into the heart of our enemies' space.

Chapter Twenty-Two

NEVIO

My phone rings. It makes me jump.

I'm not usually a jumpy person, but ever since the minute Dalila left the house I've been fidgety and agitated. I want her home.

It's only been fifteen minutes, but I am barely handling her absence and the worry is making me nauseous.

I lean over to grab my phone off the table in the living room.

Her father.

The tension in my stomach increases ten times over when I stare at his name. Why would he be calling me? Has something happened?

Thoughts fly through my mind at a million miles an hour.

"Nevio." I say with a tight throat that feels dry and scratchy.

"I thought she was supposed to be here already. She's late."

"She left fifteen minutes ago. It's only a five-minute drive." I stand up, beginning to pace.

"She's not here."

"What have you done, Vincent?" I ask, suspicious of her father.

"What the fuck does that mean?" He spits back defensively.

I slam down the phone and shout for my security guards. "She didn't reach her destination. Get in the car. We're going to find her."

I'm running towards the front of the house. My head feels as though it's going to explode. I've never felt this kind of panic before. I have never felt dread so thick like this, flooding my bones and chilling me to the core.

Two of my security personnel climb into the car with me. I pull my gun out to check the clip while we drive out of the security gate, turning in the same direction Dalila went only a short time ago.

I am scanning the roads, terrified of what I might see, constantly searching for her but also feeling a sense of hopelessness.

A short distance from the coffee shop, I can hear sirens.

The roads are congested, and we move slower through the thick traffic — until we reach the scene of an accident.

My car.

Rolled.

Smashed.

Lying on the roof, half in the road, half on the curb.

There is blood splattered down the side of the driver's door, pooling on the tar, making it shine with thick wet red liquid.

I can see the driver, but I can't see Dalila.

I push the door open and run towards the mess.

"Was there a girl?" I shout desperately at the paramedic on the scene.

"What?"

"Where is the fucking girl that was in the car?"

I only hope that she was taken in an ambulance. That this is a genuine accident.

But the look on the paramedic's face says otherwise. "There was no girl, man. Do you know this guy?"

I shake my head. Fuck. There was no girl.

Except I know there was.

"Hey, man, do you know this guy?" the paramedic screams after me as I turn away. "Dude, you have to stay and answer some questions."

But I'm already climbing back into my car, gesturing to the driver to keep going.

I need to have a word with her father.

To my surprise, he went home. He didn't go looking for her; he didn't trace her route back towards my place - he just went home.

I push my way through his front door as his security guards try to hold me back.

"Where the fuck is she?" I scream into his face, grabbing him by the collar.

Three men try to pull me off him, but I can tell they're scared of me. They know who I am. Everyone knows the stories about me.

"It's ok. It's ok." Vincent waves his security guards off me. "It's OK," He says again as they step away. I don't know if he's saying it to them or himself.

"Where is my wife, Vincent?"

"I don't know. She ever showed up."

"I know that already. We found the car. Flipped. My driver is dead, and she is missing. Now you tell me you had nothing to do with this." I am livid. Screaming. Shouting. Making an enormous noise. I never shout. I am the deadly silent shadow - but not now. Now I am a mess of fear and rage.

"What the fuck is going on?" Masaccio's voice comes from behind me and I spin towards him.

"Where is your sister?" I hiss at him.

"She's gone?" His eyes glaze over in panic. He turns towards his father. "Did you do something?" He asks.

"Why the fuck does everyone think I have something to do with this?" Vincent asks in frustration.

"Because you are the only one who knew she was traveling that route." I grab him by the collar again and shake him. He grips my wrists, trying to hold himself up, so he doesn't land flat on his face.

"Stop." Masaccio says, pulling at my arm. "That will solve nothing."

I draw my gun from my belt, staring Masaccio right in the eyes. "No, but the threat of a bullet in his head might shake his memory into action—"

Vincent screams, trying to scoot away from me. His feet slipping on the tiled floor.

"I didn't take her. I did nothing." He shouts again.

I let go of his collar, and he slams onto the floor with a thwack.

"Lenny Malone. He's the one who took her." I say coldly. "And you are going to tell me where?"

"How would I know?" He stammers, looking up at me.

Masaccio walks over to his father and pulls him to his feet.

"Nevio, we can figure this out. We'll help you."

Rufino bursts through the front door, with Celso close behind him. "What the fuck? We heard shouting." Their guns are drawn and pointed low as they stride towards us with confusion traced across their faces.

Masaccio turns towards his brothers. "Lenny Malone took Dalila." He says with disgust, staring at his father. He points his finger right into his father's face. "And you are going to tell us where he is."

"Fuck." Rufino whispers darkly. Celso's eyes are wide with horror.

I can't take this. Everyone is just staring at Vincent, waiting for him to cough up information. He has said nothing useful at all.

I watch him as he strolls over to the sofa and sits down in it, massaging his throat where I had gripped his collar. That fucker is taking his fucking time and all the while, terrible things might be happening to Dalila.

I push past Mas, who tries to block me, but not wholeheartedly. His patience is also wearing thin.

I grab Vincent by the collar again.

"Where the fuck is Lenny Malone's place?" I whisper, a hiss, a threat, a warning on my voice.

"I can show you. I can show you, for fuck's sakes. I'll show you."

Mas turns towards his brothers. "Get weapons. Call Tuomo, we are all going together. We need more men. Everyone gets their teams together."

I shake Vincent, trying to force the answer out of him. "Tell me. Now. I'm not waiting for them."

"You'll die if you go alone." He shakes his head. "He'll kill you."

"Right now your daughter is there alone - with that monster. I'm not waiting. Tell me where the fuck he is, and I will leave right now. Her brothers can catch up with me."

"Fort Larkwood. The massive property at the edge of the forest. It's an enormous house with black face bricks walls. You can't miss it."

I drop him again, this time onto the sofa, then immediately turn towards the door to leave.

Mas blocks me, only for a moment.

One look in my eyes and he knows not to even bother trying.

He takes a deep breath and steps out of my way. "We'll be right behind you." He says after me.

My two security guards climb back into the car with me and I punch the location onto the map system. It's worthy five minutes away.

With all of this chaos, all of this wasted time, she is probably there already.

Fuck knows what he is doing to her or what he has planned for her.

"Break the speed limits. Not of them matter." I say as my driver pressed his foot heavy against the accelerator.

Snow beats against the windscreen, slowing us down. I swear under my breath.

I've done dark things in my life.

I know I'm a monster.

But nothing I have done in the past is going to compare to what I will do to Malone if he has laid his hands on my wife.

Chapter Twenty-Three

DALILA

The back of his hand stings against my face as he slaps me again.

Blood trickles in a slow, lazy drip from my split lip.

I lick it, tasting the metallic flavor of iron.

My eyes flutter as they try to stay open.

My body is shivering. I am freezing cold, in shock, in pain - I don't know which one is causing me to shiver - perhaps all of them. My vision swims in and out of focus.

Suddenly the air is beaten from my lungs as a heavy boot kicks into my ribs.

"Answer me, you little bitch." The man leaning over me spits at me. It hits the ground in front of me and I watch it spread, mixing with my blood that has pooled through.

"I don't know." I breathe, my ribs aching.

"Fuck." He screams and slaps me again. His knuckle connects with my eye and pain burns through to the bone.

My head drops backwards. I can barely hold it up anymore.

I close my eyes as my consciousness drifts away from me.

Someone grabs my jaw.

The man.

It must be Lenny Malone. His expensive suit and shiny shoes are too nice for security. His air of arrogance and unrestrained cruelty - it can only be him.

"This fucking bitch will talk. She just needs a little more motivation. Strip her down. Let her relax here in the basement for an hour or two without the heating on."

"She won't last that long."

"We'll see about that."

"It's freezing down here."

"If she dies - it'll just be a lesson for her father. Don't fuck with me. Don't make me promises you don't intend to keep."

Malone turns his back on me, and I squint, trying to focus on the other men around me.

Hands tug at my already torn clothing. Pulling them off my body. I wince and try to kick them away, but they are rough, heartless, and cruel. Within moments, I am in nothing but my lace panties. My naked skin pressed against the concrete floor. I glance down at my body as I try to wrap my arms around myself. I can already see the bruises beginning to color. Bright and dark blue marks etched into my skin.

I press my hand over a cut on my side, the impact of a boot split my skin open.

My body is shaking even more now. I dare not say anything.

I know this man is not the reason. Nothing I say is going to help my situation.

I don't even know what he wants from me. I don't know what information he is trying to get.

The men all walk away from me. One by one, they turn their backs on me as though I was a stray dog they didn't care about. As though I was nothing, no one, worthless and useless. Because, after all, that is what I am to them.

The massive light above me flickers, clicks and goes out.

Darkness.

My fears coming to life as the shadows in every corner make shapes. Creeping towards me.

I shift, moving in painfully slow motions to the center of the floor. Where the only bit of light is still touching.

Pale blue light is filtering through the small windows near the ceiling. Those windows are at ground level outside, but in here they are high above me.

Pale blue snow tinted light.

It makes the space look colder. It feels empty and threatening - that pale light - void of life.

But at least it softens the edges of the darkness. I don't know what I would do if there was only darkness.

I am terrified of the dark.

I lay in the cold shadows on the concrete floor of Lenny Malone's basement and cry. My body is shivering that my muscles feel like they are spasming in pain.

I roll onto my side as I pull my legs up against my chest, wrapping my arms around them to hold myself in the smallest ball I can. Trying to keep my warmth, what little of it I have.

My father sold me to this man.

He sold me to this man so that he wouldn't have to go to jail for a few years.

He thought that this torture, this pain, this degrading treatment - this absolute cruelty - was a fair trade for him staying free.

My lips are numb as the coldness creeps deeper into my body.

I can feel death looking over my shoulder. Whispering sweet promises in my ear.

Soon it won't hurt anymore.

Soon you can close your eyes and forget about this pain.

"I don't want to die." I whisper back, my voice startling me.

The tears that run over my cheeks feel warm. They remind me I'm not dead yet.

I can't die. Because I want to see him again.

I want to lie in his arms and hear him say my name. I want to see the way the corners of his lips curl up and create those gorgeous dimples in his cheeks.

I want to trace my fingers over the devil's mark on his body, the jagged edges embossed into his skin forever.

I close my eyes, but I feel my body drifting, as though death is disguised as sleep.

I can't sleep now. I might never wake up.

Blinking into the dark, I try to sit up, but my body is in so much pain I'm finding it impossible. I can hardly move my hands, never mind anything else.

"Nevio." I whisper into the darkness. "Please come and find me before it's too late."

My tears feel frozen on my cheeks. I can't even reach up to touch them because my hands are too sore.

"Please, I can't do this - I need you."

Chapter Twenty-Four

NEVIO

It feels as though the snow is against us as it coats the roads and makes the drive treacherous.

The forest looms on either side of the road, thick cold mist dancing through the trunks of those tall pines - it makes the place look ominous.

On any other day, it might have been beautiful.

But my mind is in dark places.

I turn my face away from the line of trees, back towards the road. The driver is going along the slippery tar at a reasonable speed, but I am still annoyed.

"Can't we go any faster?" I snarl.

"Not if you want to get there. If we go any faster, we will slide and roll, and Dalila will be on her own."

I shut my mouth. I know he's right, but it still pisses me off.

"How long until we get there?"

"At this speed, less than twenty minutes."

Ok. That's not so bad. Less than twenty minutes and then I can take this frustration and anger out on someone. I hate keeping it bottled inside like this.

I will turn on the man who has taken from me the thing I love most in this world.

In the back of the car, I hear my other security guard checking his weapon.

We all feel tense.

Lenny Malone is a dangerous man. A savage.

We might very well lose our lives this afternoon.

I dial Mas.

The phone rings a few times before he answers. I can hear his car. They are already on their way.

"We'll be there in the next fifteen minutes."

"Alright. Then we will be about fifteen or thirty minutes behind you, depending on this snow."

"You left sooner than I expected." I say with relief. I am grateful to have the backup so close.

"You should wait for us to get there. It'll be better if we all go in at the same time." He suggests.

"I can't. That's fifteen or twenty minutes in which anything could happen to her. I can't take that risk."

"We'll see you there then. As soon as we can."

For the last stretch of the drive, I hardly notice the scenery. My mind is chaos.

I've never done a job that I was so emotionally invested in. Every time I've gone after someone, it was just a paid project. A simple mission. There was no piece of my heart or soul in it. This is so different.

This means everything to me, and I'm stressed.

I take a deep breath. I have to focus. I can't be so disshelved. The more emotionless I am, the more successful I will be.

But it's impossible. I can't switch off my worry, or my fears, or the hatred I have for the man who took her. I can't stop how much I love her.

It's impossible.

I'll just have to use that chaos to my advantage.

"We're coming up on the building now, sir."

I squint ahead of us and see the dark shape of a massive black house silhouetted against the misty trees behind it.

Fuck. It's cold.

That place looks like the entrance to hell.

"Park just to the edge there. Don't go all the way. We'll walk the rest on foot. Hopefully, they are too arrogant to be expecting us this soon."

"Yes, sir." The driver confirms, pulling off the road into the dirt.

"Our mission is simple. Find Dalila. Kill whoever gets in the way."

I see fear in the driver's eyes when he glances at me.

"Reinforcements are only fifteen minutes behind us. Do as much as you can until they get here. And stay alive."

He nods, looking uncertain.

I know I'm asking a lot for them to follow me into the house of the most monstrous man in the city -

I sigh.

"I understand if this is not something you are willing to do. I can go in by myself."

"Not a fuck." Comes the unison reply from both of them. "Sir, I might be shitting myself, but I'm going in with you."

"Same for me." From the backseat.

I smile.

"Thank you."

We walk along the edge of the forest, feeling the damp air against our skin, staying low in the misty coverage.

At the corner of the black house, we climb the iron fencing. Silently moving like water over rocks.

My feet touch the earth on the inside of his property. Next to me, a soft thud as two security guards drop to the ground as well.

I gesture for them to follow me. It's better if we stay together.

Before we even look for a way in, we move around the outside perimeter.

Our knives slicing into the flesh of anyone we come across. Bodies lay in our wake, bleeding, lifeless and without even a call for help from one of them.

No one was expecting us.

"Are you ready?" I ask in a whisper.

They nod.

I push on the front door, and it swings open.

Moving like the shadow I am, I am inside the house before they can even blink. One guard, down on his knees, clutching at his throat. Another hears the wet gurgle and comes running, but he's taken down by my security before he can even reach me.

I motion either direction of the giant staircase and we move through the house until finally I find Malone.

In the bath, soaking in steaming water. A naked woman sitting on his lap.

At first I think it's her.

But that's just fear - because this girl has dark hair.

My gun clicks as I cock it and Malone spins around in shock.

The girl screams, and water splashes over the edge of the tub as she scoots off him.

Malone laughs.

I fire and a bullet pierces right through his arm, shattering a hole in the wall behind him.

"What the fuck?" He screams in pain. Clutch at his arm as blood oozes through his fingers into the tub.

The girl looks horrified and tries to climb out as red stains the water, drifting towards her. "Don't you dare move." I warn her. "Malone. If you would kindly get out."

I hear gunshots from somewhere in the house as my men continue to work their way through the space.

"I wasn't expecting anyone." Malone says, slipping and grabbing the edge of the bath as he climbs out.

"I noticed. Your security was — lacking, to say the least."

"My security is never lacking. There were over twenty men out there." He says, sounding bitter.

"Twenty three and counting."

"Hmph." He grabs a towel and wraps it around his waist. I watch every movement he makes like a hawk - I don't want any surprises.

"Where is she?" I ask calmly.

The woman in the tub, still staring in shock at the blood in the water, looks up at Malone. "She? What does he mean - *she*?" She spits at him. "Are you fucking around again?" She screams bitterly.

"Shut up, Melissa. For fuck sakes." He snarls at her.

"If there is another woman, I swear to - "

He lifts his hand towards her, and she flinches, ducking low in the water.

"Enough." I say.

I point the gun at Melissa, but don't take my eyes off Malone. "Where does he keep prisoners, sweetheart?" I ask, with darkness on the edge of my voice.

"Oh fuck, don't shoot me, oh fuck—"

"You have five seconds."

"The basement." She blurts out.

Malone shakes his head. "Fucking bitch."

"Walk." I command and Malone pads his way down the stairs towards the basement. I follow with my gun aimed at his head.

We are halfway down the stairs when the front door opens, and men pour inside. At first I am ready to shoot, but then I see the familiar faces.

Mas, Rufino, Celso, Toum0, and Vincent. Their guards all armed to the tea.

"You didn't even leave any for us," Mas says, looking around.

Malone grumbles. "Can I put on some clothes? I didn't know I was going to have guests today."

"Shut the fuck up and keep walking." I shove him.

The guards stay behind, and her father and brothers follow me down the steep flight of stone steps into the dark, musty smelling basement.

My eyes struggle to adjust to the darkness.

But is that her? It can't be?

It looks like a pile of skin and bones laying in the center of the floor.

"Lights." I shout in anger as my eyes adjust and I see the definite curve of her hip. Her body is so familiar to me now.

I'm running towards her, dropping to my knees, pain clutching at my heart as I pull her into my arms.

She is freezing cold, her body feels lifeless, blood is coating her skin and the ground beneath her. The sticky familiarity of it making me feel ill at this moment.

"Dalila." I shout, touching her face, shaking her gently. "Dalila."

The lights flicker to life above me and they light the genuine horror of what she looks like.

Thick dark bruises are coating her skin, deep cuts, swollen eyes, blood - so much blood.

She is practically blue. She is so cold.

"Is she breathing?" Celso is on his knees next to me, tears in his eyes. "Is she fucking breathing?"

Mas has Malone on his knees, begging for his life at the sight of her brother's rage directed at him. "What the fuck did you do to her?" He screams into Malone's face.

She jolts awake, and instantly her face is flooded with pain. She winces in my arms and I drag her against my chest, rocking her. "Dalila, it's me. It's Nev. I found you. It's going to be ok." She is shaking uncontrollably.

I stand up, lifting her with me, gripping her. Celso pulls his jacket off and helps me wrap it over her shoulders. He looks distraught.

Her father is peering at her, tears streaming down his cheeks.

"I didn't know. I didn't know." He keeps repeating, over and over again.

"I didn't know."

I stare at him with hatred. "You knew." I snarl.

I walk over to where Masaccio has Malone groveling.

Cradling Dalila in one arm, I pull my gun from my belt and aim it at his head.

I want to pull the trigger, but it seems too easy. Too quick.

I want him to suffer.

"Handcuff him to the bolt on the floor. It's there where Dalila was lying."

Was drags Malone over to the bolt and cuffs him to it. He grabs the man's towel and yanks it off his body, leaving him naked, his skin against the cold cement, already coated in Dalila's blood from the floor.

"Leave him there."

"Wait, no - please - " he begs. "It's freezing in here. I'll be dead in thirty minutes."

Mas nods at me. "I'll stay. I want to make sure he's dead before I leave."

"Message me. When it's over."

Malone screams. "You can't do this. I'll kill you all. It's too fucking cold. I'm going to die, you fucking animals."

I turn my back on his panic.

I carry Lila up at the stairs, out of the house that looks like the gates to hell.

I climb into the back seat of the car with her still wrapped in my arms, holding her in my lap.

"The doctor is waiting for you at home, baby girl." I whisper against her hair.

Chapter Twenty-Five

DALILA

I remember seeing Nevio's face. I remember the moment he lifted me in his arms.

I knew he had come to save me - but the two or three days that came after that were a blur.

This morning is the first time I remember opening my eyes and seeing my bed.

I sit up, moving too fast as pain shoots through me.

"Nev." I scream, terrified, flashes of Malone's face shooting through my mind.

He comes running into the room. He grabs me in his arms, and I cry out in pain again.

"Sorry. I'm sorry. What happened? Are you ok?" he blurts.

"I - I - I don't know what happened. I don't know how I got here." I mumbled in shock.

"You've been really out of it since I brought you home. The doctor has been seeing you twice a day. We've just been waiting for you to wake up."

"You found me—" I whisper, tears falling down my cheeks.

"Of course I found you. There is no way in hell that I would not find you, my baby girl." He rocks me gently in his arms and I rest my face against his chest.

After a quiet moment, he asks. "Do you remember what happened - while you were there?"

I nod.

"You remember what he did to you?" His voice is tight.

I nod again.

"Did he - " He can't finish his sentence, but I know what he is worried about.

"No." I whisper. "He - " but now I can't finish my sentence. My throat closes over the words I want to say.

Nevio waits, holding me.

"He beat me. He - he hurt me."

"I know sweet, baby girl. I know. And he paid for that."

"Is he dead?" I ask with bitter anger. I want him to be dead. I want him to have felt pain and met death in the same way he left me to suffer.

"We left him chained to the basement floor wearing nothing. He froze was dead within thirty-seven minutes. He screamed and begged for mercy, bt he found none."

I nod, satisfied, feeling like some kind of justice was served.

Nevio leans away from me to look at my face.

"The swelling is going down nicely. Are you hungry? Do you want coffee or hot chocolate? What do you need?"

My stomach flips and growls loudly in response. I laugh. It's a weird sound after everything I've been through, but it brings me comfort to still feel a smile on my face.

"Hot chocolate. And a burger and fries." I grin. It hurts my lip.

"A burger and fries?" he asks, surprised.

I nod.

With a chuckle, Nevio gestures to the man standing just outside my door.

"Please arrange two burgers and fries and some hot chocolate." He asks, then turns towards me. "I'm staying right here." He lifts the covers and kicks his shoes off so that he can crawl into bed with me. I snuggle against his chest, trying not to touch my bruised side.

"What did the doctor say?" I ask, wondering how injured I really am because my body feels like I was dragged behind a truck for ten miles.

"One broken rib, fourteen stitches, and some deep bruising. He says the rib will take the longest to heal, but luckily it's a hairline fracture. You need to rest for two weeks. You're allowed to walk around, but mostly sleep - good food and a lot of cuddles."

"The doctor recommended cuddles?" I giggle.

"No, I might have added that part in myself." He pulls me closer to his body.

I feel him take a deep breath, his chest rising and falling.

"Lila - I was so scared. When I found out you were taken. I have never been that scared in my life." He swallows. "I'm so sorry I didn't find you sooner."

"I knew you would find me, Nev." I say calmly, looking up at him and seeing the pain in his eyes. "I never doubted it."

He smiles, and the warmth of it lights his face.

I close my eyes again.

"Baby girl, your father has been around to see you every day since we found you. Yesterday he came over twice, wanting to see you. I haven't let him in the house. I wanted you to make that choice. It isn't mine to make."

I shake my head. "I don't want to see him."

"He was there when we found you. He saw you - I think that only in that moment did he realize—"

"I don't want to see him." I repeat angrily.

I feel Nev's hand brush through my hair. "I understand." He says. "I won't allow him into the house."

The week that followed, I felt more like myself. I walked around the house, slept a lot, ate a lot, rested in Nevio's arms a lot - and kept saying no every time my father came to the house.

The bruises faded to dark brownish yellow marks and eventually disappeared altogether.

At two weeks, the doctor removed my stitches and told me my rib was healing very well.

My body was getting stronger and healthy again, but my heart was still raging about what my father did.

Late one night, sitting on the sofa in the living room with a thick blanket wrapped around me as I lean against Nevio, I am thinking about my father.

The fire crackles loudly, warding off the heavy snow that is piling up on the ground outside.

"Winter is here." Nevio says, hugging me against his body. My back is resting on his chest, his arms around my stomach.

"It's really beautiful." I reply, but my mind is elsewhere.

"Are you ok, Lila? I can see your skin is beautiful, your stitches are gone, you are moving with almost no pain - but your eyes are still distant."

"I've been thinking a lot about my father. I think, now that I have seen with my own eyes what he traded me into, I think I hate him. I don't want to hate him, though. It hurts me to have hate for my father."

Nevio is quiet for a while, then he talks gently.

"You don't hate him. You are angry with him - and you have every right to be. At the moment, it's how you need to feel - and you should feel. Don't stop yourself from feeling what you need to feel. When the time is right, those feelings might change. You might soften a little. Don't feel bad for being angry with him, baby girl."

Hearing him say that I am allowed to feel the way I feel is like someone lifting a heavy weight off my shoulders. Was beating myself up for hating my father, but he's right. I can be angry. I have a right to feel this way.

I take a deep breath. How is it he always knows exactly how to soothe my worries and make me feel better?

I turn in his arms so that I am lying with my chin resting on his chest as I look up at him.

"Thank you." I whisper.

And I mean it with all my heart.

"Thank you for coming to rescue me and thank you for taking care of me afterwards - and thank you - for understanding my heart."

He cups his hand around my chin and presses his lips against mine.

"I will always be here for you, baby girl. No matter what happens."

Chapter Twenty-Six

NEVIO

Dalila is fully healed, and that bright, beautiful smile is back on her face.

She is laughing again, and the house feels more and more like a home with her around.

I grin as I think about the surprise I have planned for her. I'm taking her somewhere special tonight. She thinks we are just going out to dinner, but actually, I have something very different planned.

It's five and I'm nervous as I wait for her downstairs in my crisp black suit.

When I see her at the top of the staircase, my stomach flips with tension. How the fuck does she look even more beautiful every single time I see her? How is this possible?

She stands there, smiling down at me, her lips painted red to match the red dress she has chosen to wear tonight. Her black heals and glitter black clutch complimenting everything perfectly.

She has her hair half pinned up in a sort of messy style that has left curls hanging around her face.

I watch as she walks slowly towards me, taking each step carefully because her eyes keep returning to meet mine.

When she reaches the ground floor, she reaches out and pulls herself against me. "Wow." She says, as her eyes take me in. "You look so freaking sexy." She laughs. "We don't have to go out, you know, we can stay home and - " She grins mischievously.

"Oh no, temptress, we are going out. Don't think you can lure me back to bed with that gorgeous look - although it is working - "

I shut my eyes. "No. Stop look at me with those eyes. Get your ass outside and get into the car." I demand, pointing towards the front door and refusing to look at her.

I hear her giggle and then the sound of her heels on the floor as she walks towards the door.

I grin and touch the thing in my pocket, making sure it's still there.

Outside, the driver is holding the door open for me, waiting for me. I slide into the seat next to Dalila.

She shifts closer to me and runs her hands over my thigh.

"Where are we going?" She asks, not for the first time. She's been trying to find out for three days already.

"I told you. For dinner."

"Yes, I know, but where?" She whines and laughs at the same time.

"It's a place with a hell of a view." I grin, giving away a clue.

"Oh - that restaurant at the top of the tallest building in town? I love that place." She says.

I shake my head. "No."

"Nev." She huffs, but I can tell she is loving this.

Instead of turning towards town, the driver turns left once he is out of our property. Dalila's eyes narrow towards me. I say nothing at all.

We drive for around half an hour, making small talk, while she holds back her urge to ask me again.

"Nev - " She says in frustration. "When are you going - "

"We're here." I grin as the car turns off the road down a gravel side path, the tires crunching on the dirt road.

"Where?" she says in confusion, looking around and seeing nothing at all.

The car keeps heading down the road.

Towards a parking lot.

The driver stops and opens the door for us.

I hold my hand out, and Lila takes it in hers to steady herself on the uneven ground.

"I'm not wearing the right outfit for a hike." She glares at me, still smiling, though.

"That's why I brought these for you." The driver hands me a pair of black high-top sneakers covered in black crystals. They shine in late sunlight.

"Sit, I'll help you put them on."

"Those are gorgeous." She says. Admiring her new shoes. She pulls her high heels off and leaves them in the car while I slip a pair of socks into her feet, followed by the new shoes.

She jumps out of the car, looking even more beautiful in the long red dress and the sneakers. She looks like she's ready for an adventure.

I hold out my hand. "Come on."

Leading her to the edge of the parking lot, we stand looking down on a massive field - and in it there is an air balloon - just about to be inflated.

She squeals with excitement and jumps up into my arms.

"Are you serious? I've always wanted to go on one of these." She shouts, then pulls me down the hill towards the massive, colorful balloon.

We watch in awe as it inflates and grows bigger and bigger.

Finally, we climb into the basket and start rising into the air.

The balloon drifts upwards into the glowing orange and pink sky, streaks of purple splashing between the clouds. The air is icy up here.

I lean down and pick up the jackets. I had them put in the basket for us.

She shakes her head, smiling. "You thought of everything."

We stand at the edge of the basket, looking across the sky, drift through it like we belong up here, alone - away from the rest of the world.

I wrap my arms around her as she leans her back against my chest. I can see she is smiling when I look down at her.

"Lila."

"Mm?" she says, glancing up at me. Pulling her eyes away from the view.

"There is something I've been wanting to tell you for a long time. I just wanted to wait, until you were better, and now—well, now you are."

I take a deep breath. She turns to look at me, the pink sky turning a touch of purple and reflecting in her eyes.

"I'm in love with you. I am so madly and deeply in love with you, I don't even want to think of a time when you aren't in my life."

A wide, warm smile spreads across her face. "You love me?"

"I do, baby girl."

She drops her eyes as her dark lashes flutter. When she looks up at me again, she looks nervous. "I love you too, Nevio. I have for a while and I didn't want to tell you and make you feel weird about it."

I chuckle.

"You love me?"

"More than the world, more than words, more than anything."

I drop to my knee, pulling the ring out of my pocket.

"I know we are already married, but the first time - it wasn't done the way I would have wanted - will you marry me - again?"

She squeals with laughter and happiness and leaps into my arms. I am knocked off my feet as she lands on me, giggling and kissing me all over my face.

"Yes. Yes. Yes. Yes. Yes." she says between each kiss.

The basket of the air balloon is swinging a little when I pull her back up to her feet.

"So, that's a yes, then?" I ask, teasing her.

She nods. "It's the biggest yes ever."

I lift her hand and slip the new ring onto her finger. It fits right alongside her existing ring. I don't want to change how we met. I don't want to erase it or cancel it. I just want to add to it.

"So, we are going to plan our wedding together then?" I ask, wondering if she's one of those girls that have been dreaming about what her dress will look like since she was in kindergarten.

"Everything. I want to plan everything with you."

She snuggles against me as we continue to drift through the air.

When we do finally find ourselves back on the ground, there is a big white tent set up with a fire going inside, making the entire tent glow with warmth. There is a table set up inside for a private dinner and fairy lights have been strung over the roof of the tent.

I pull her into the tent and sit her down at the small, intimate table.

The chef brings out her favorite food - Salmon - prepared a little differently this time, crumbed and baked.

The night drifts on and we spend hours talking and laughing and eating until it's too late to keep our eyes open and I lift her in my arms and carry her to the back of the tent where a beautiful king sized bed awaits us.

Chapter Twenty-Seven

DALILA

We have been having an amazing time planning our second wedding. This time our families and friends will be there - it will be a massive event because we want to celebrate of marriage with everyone we know.

I want to scream that I love him from every rooftop in the city.

I am so happy. My heart is so full of life and love.

Nevio steps close to me as we stand on the step outside my brother's house. I asked Mas to arrange a family dinner for me and to invite everyone - including my father.

I take a deep breath.

"Are you ok?" Nev asks, squeezing my hand.

"I'm ok. I'm ready."

I nod, forcing myself to feel confident enough to handle this.

I decided about a week ago.

The realization came to me one night when I was lying on Nevio's chest, listening to his breathing while he slept.

Everything has happened for a reason. And I would not change a single moment of it. Even the parts that were terrifying. The parts were I was furious at my family. The parts where I thought my own brothers had betrayed me. The part where my father betrayed me.

Even the part where I almost lost my life.

I wouldn't change any of it because all of it is the reason that I met Nevio.

If my father hadn't messed up, my brother would not have bet me off in a poker game - a game where Nevio was playing.

If I hadn't been forced into it, I would never have given him a chance, and that fills my heart with shame because he is the most beautiful, loving, and gentlemanly person to me.

He is the perfect person for me.

That one night a week ago, I realized I should thank my father for messing up.

He is the reason I am married to Nevio - the shadow monster. The one who has the devil's mark.

I shake my head, thinking about how crazy it has all been, but there is a smile on my face when I walk into my brother's house.

The smell of roasted lamb and crispy roast potatoes fills the air.

The holiday season is almost over, but the family spirit is high in this house.

Red sees me first and comes out to pull me into a hug.

"Baby sister. You look good."

He shakes Nevio's hand, towering over him. No one is taller than Red.

"Rufino, good to see you, man."

Mas and Celso come say hello next, then Tuomo.

Tuomo grins at me. "Are we going to witness you giving dad any lectures tonight?" He chuckles.

"Oh stop. I don't want any drama tonight." I punch him in the shoulder, and he fakes an injury just as well as the soccer players do.

Nev and I walk through the house towards the living room. Mas hands us each a drink when we enter. Gin for me and whiskey for Nev.

My father is sitting on the sofa near the patio doors. He stands up, looking unsure about whether he can come over and say hello.

I let go of Nev's hand, and he throws me an encouraging smile.

I walk right up to my father. Holding my head high. Smiling, but feeling weary in my heart.

"Dad."

"Lila." He says, nervous and tense.

"Here." I hand him a pearl white envelope. The paper has a shimmer to it that catches the light when you move it. He doesn't notice the shimmer as he stares down at the embossed outline of his name on the front. "What is this?"

"Open it." I say, gesturing my hand towards it.

His jaw muscles clench and unclench as he works the top of the envelope free. Folding it back, he dips his fingers inside to grab the pieces of folded paper.

He slides it out and places it on top of the envelope, unfolding it, glancing up at me as his eyes catch mine.

I see the thick tension running in the lines across his aged face.

He looks back down at the unfolded piece of paper and breathes a heavy sigh of relief.

You are invited to join us on our wedding day - to celebrate this special moment with us.

He swallows back his emotions and pulls me into his arms.

I lean against him, not hugging back, but also not pushing him away.

What he did still causes me a great deal of pain, but I need to let it go, and move on.

I need to be grateful for the good that came out of it rather than focusing on the trauma.

My dad lets me go and looks into my eyes.

"Thank you, sweetheart. I will be there." He nods, then folds the paper back and slips it into his jacket pocket. Patting it once.

Sitting at the table, I look around at my brothers.

"Hey, guys, when is at least one of you going to get a girlfriend, so I don't have to be the only woman at these things?" I huff in annoyance, lifting my hands in the air dramatically.

They all laugh.

"We have a bet that Mas will be the first to get a girl." Celso says.

"Bullshit. When do I have time for women? I am not interested in that drama." Mas shakes his head, adamant that he is not the type of man who falls in love.

Celso laughs and points at Tuomo. "The other twin then." He states. Tuomo throws him a glare that might be sharper than daggers.

His icy stare has Celso shifting in his seat and then rolling his eyes.

Mas chuckles. "It'll be Red."

"Oh please, he's a fucking giant. He'd trample any woman that tried to date him." I say imagining some tiny girl next to the family giant.

Red lets a low growl escape his lips as he picks up his dinner knife and points it at Mas.

I giggle and glance over at Nev. He laughs and shakes his head, then slips his hand beneath the table and runs it over my leg. He leans close to me as the boys continue to fight over this ridiculous topic.

"I'm the luckiest man alive, you know."

I lean back to look into his eyes. A massive grin touches my lips. "Oh, I know." I say cheekily.

Later that night we are on our way home when Nev reaches out and takes my hand, not taking his eyes off the road, though.

"Lila."

"Yes?" I look over at him, enjoying the view of his profile against the streetlights outside the car window.

"Why did you forgive your father? What helped you decide that?"

I smile, letting my eyes drop to my lap. "You."

"Me?" he glances over at me.

"You. Because everything that I went through because of my father's horrible choices - his selfish actions - all of it led to me meeting you. IF he hadn't done that, I wouldn't be married to you. I wouldn't have had that chance."

"But—what Malone did to you—surely—"

"It was all worth it, Nev. Every moment. Everything that happened. If I knew I could have you, I would go through all of it again."

He shakes his head as a deep frown carves into his forehead.

"For me?"

He doesn't believe me.

I laugh and reach out to touch his face.

"You are everything to me." I whisper, tracing my finger over his jaw.

Chapter Twenty-Eight

NEVIO

The morning is absolute chaos.

The house is packed, there are people everywhere, all rushing in different directions, making a noise, shouting, laughing, drinking.

I need to get everyone out of here and to the venue within an hour.

I stand in the middle of my living room, unsure of what to do next.

Lucia brushes past me, then steps back to me. "There you are. Gosh, I've been looking everywhere. Ok good, you're dressed."

"Where is Dalila? Aren't you supposed to be helping her get ready?"

"Yes, dumbass. I am helping her. I just came to tell you we are heading through to the hotel at the venue. Are you going to get all of her brothers there in one piece?" She looks around at the chaos, her eyes wide. "It's odd, isn't it - that this wedding seems more crazy than the first time you married her?"

I chuckle. "It does, right?"

"Ok, well, we are leaving. Don't be late."

She disappears, and I shove my hands in my pockets. I'll be there on time. I don't have a singled doubt about that. But Tuomo and Red have been taking tequila shots and I'm wondering if they are going to make it.

Although, they both look like they are handling it just fine.

I sigh.

Mas comes up next to me, gripping my arm.

"Relax man. Don't worry about this mess. I'll sort everything out here. If you want to go ahead to the venue, you can. I'll make sure the caterers are ready for our return party."

"You sure?" I ask, because I really, really want to get out of here. There are too many people and there is too much going on.

"I'm sure. Go."

With relief I leave the house, grabbing my tuxedo jacket on the way to the car.

I cannot wait to marry her again. And I want this to be the most special day for her — but I hate all of this attention.

I just want her to be happy. I want to celebrate with her. And I know she is loving every moment of this day. She's been excited about it for weeks.

I pull out my phone in the car and message her.

> Me: I'm thinking about you. I can't wait to see you.

>> Lila: I'm so excited. I love my dress and my flowers. I love everything about today. Can't wait to marry you again.

> Me: Is my sister being a pain in the ass or is she helping you?

>> Lila: You'll never believe it. She kept the penny - from our first wedding. I left it in her shoe, and she found it and she kept it. It's in my shoe again.

I chuckle. Lucia really is sentimental. I'll have to have that coin framed.

> Me: A Six pence for your shoe. Keep it safe. It's been with us since the beginning.

> Lila: And forever.

The church is overflowing with guests when the organ music plays.

A hushed silence falls across the room as everyone turns towards the doors.

Lila steps inside in the most beautiful dress ever.

It hugs her waist, flaring out around her like a soft cloud, moving and swirling over her body like waves caressing the shoreline.

The sleeveless bodice hugs her, accentuating her feminine, delicate shoulders, and that gorgeous plunging cleavage.

She walks towards me with the veil covering her face.

Memories flash through me.

The night I married her.

My heart always knew it was her.

I had no doubts, and now, seeing her walking towards me again, I know it all over again.

She was always meant to be mine.

This world knew the moment she was born that she would one day belong to me.

After the ceremony, there is a rather wild and fun party at our home.

The food is incredible; the champagne is flowing, and the guests are having the most amazing time.

I pull Lila up against me as we move on the dance floor set up in our garden. The massive white tents are filled with people and warmth.

"This day was perfect." She grins up at me.

"It was perfect. But it's not over yet." I say.

"Are you sure? I'm exhausted and I can't wait for everyone to go home." She laughs and then looks around to check that no one heard.

"Who says we have to wait? Do you think they will even notice if we sneak off now and go to bed?"

"Nevio. Are you serious?" She grins, hoping I am.

I lift her in my arms. It's past midnight and most of the people are too tipsy to care, anyway.

I carry her past the groups of people, talking and enjoying themselves, up the stairs, to our bedroom.

I close the door, locking it behind me.

She walks over to the bed, her back to me.

"I can't take this off by myself." She glances over her shoulder.

"Perhaps we should leave it on, then? You look beautiful in it."

"Wait till you see what's underneath."

My heart beats wildly in my chest. I step behind her and drag the invisible zip down over her spine, over the curve of her ass. The wedding dress falls open and drifts down her body onto the floor around her feet.

I clench my jaw.

"Holy fuck." I mutter, staring at her, letting my eyes take in the most heavenly sight.

"Do you like it?" she asks innocently, running her hands over the sheer white lace that barely hides any part of her at all, but somehow teases my body in ways I didn't know was possible.

"Like it?" I shake my head. "No. I absolutely love it." I grab her and pull her against me. She gasps in fright as I bend down, threading my arm through her legs, grabbing her ass, and lifting her off her feet.

"Oh, my word." She squeals as I toss her onto the bed.

Then I grab her ankle and drag her closer to me again.

"Play with yourself." I demand, looking down at her as I unbutton my shirt.

She bites her lower lip, sending shivers through me. I watch as her hand drifts over her stomach and between her legs. Her lips part as she brushes her delicate fingers over her pussy.

She gasps.

I yank my belt off and her eyes are on my cock, waiting for me to pull my pants down so that she can see. She's hungry for me.

I watch her, my eyes drifting over the suspends holding up the white fishnets - she pulls her white lace panties to the side and dips her fingers inside herself.

My cock throbs.

I step out of my pants, naked, standing over her.

I lay on the bed, breathing in her scent, feeling the heat of her body.

"It's my turn." I growl as I spread her legs wide and push my cock inside her.

She cries out with pleasure, and I fuck her. I'm not gentle. This is not our first time together. I know what she wants.

I thrust into her, deep and hard, pushing her hips wider and opening her pussy all the way as I penetrate her.

The moans she is making are so loud our guests might hear, but clearly neither of us cares.

I fuck her until her legs are shaking, and her back is arching against me.

"Look at me when you come, baby girl." Her eyes lock with mine as waves of pleasure pulse through her and her pussy clamps over my cock.

I explode inside her, growling.

We lay in each other's arms, smiling.

She rolls over to look into my eyes.

"I love you, Nevio Armano." She whispers.

"I love you, Dalila Armano." I whisper back, then press my lips against hers so that I can taste her again.

About the Author

Hannah Rio is from a small town where she grew up reading romance books sent monthly by her book club. She developed a flair for crafting intricate love stories. She understands the delicate dance of heartbreak and joy. As a storyteller, she enjoys contemporary romances with strong, ambitious leading characters working through life's unexpected twists.

Her female and male characters can make hearts flutter and eyes tear up. Her novels promise to bring readers back to continue events of new love and passion, secrets, surprises, painful memories, sassy and sweet, grumpy or good-hearted, and adventures with happy ever after endings.

Sign up to her newsletter here:

https://dl.bookfunnel.com/slno67x24w

- instagram.com/hannahrio2024
- amazon.com/author/hannahrio
- linkedin.com/in/hannah-rio-218707307

Also by Hannah Rio

BILLIONAIRES & BABY DADDY'S

Billionaire Baby Daddy Dilemma

Off-Limits Silver Fox Boss

MAFIA MEN

Vece Familia Series

Something Old

Something New

Something Borrowed

Something Blue

Printed in Great Britain
by Amazon